BETTER

LATE

THAN

NEVER

John Potter

Published 2003 by The Arnold Bennett Society
106 Scotia Road, Burslem, Stoke-on-Trent, ST6 4ET

Copyright 2001   John Potter

Cover design by John Potter

Printed by Moor Print, Manaton (01647) 221229

ISBN 0 9537202 1 7

To my grand-daughter Yasmine Jessica, with love,
in the hope that she will grow up to appreciate
the joys of reading

BETTER LATE THAN NEVER

AUTHOR'S NOTE

When I retired one of my plans was to try and become a writer of sorts. After eight years I have made some progress, having written (in some cases in partnership) several books of which three have actually been published. At an early stage I resigned myself to the fact that I should never be able to write creatively. Research, collation and factual stuff - yes, but fiction - sadly not. In any case, a great deal of my time came to be devoted to community work and to the Arnold Bennett Society. Then, one sleepless night (a frequent happening when there are problems to be solved) I suddenly found myself with a storyline running through my head, followed closely by start and finish lines. In the morning I sat down and simply wrote a short story, and during the next few days others followed almost naturally.

I was flabbergasted but, of course, delighted, and this book is the result of a few months' work in a field to which I had never in my wildest sleepless nights expected to gain admission.

I assume that most writers of fiction start by using their own experiences and memories as a basis for their storylines; certainly in the works of many famous authors a strong autobiographical streak is plainly visible. These stories are no exception, but I must admit to borrowing an occasional trait or quality (always a good one) from an individual person whom it has been my privilege to know ; however, I have deliberately kept in-depth characteristics to a minimum. The events and circumstances are different, for many of these do come from first-hand knowledge or personal experience, and I hope that if anyone recognises some event in which they were involved, they will excuse me on the grounds of my belief that realism is a most important part of fiction, and that even fantasy is human action and reaction, simply reset in a different environment.

For me this has been a long time coming, but - Better Late than Never.

John Potter,   November 2001

BETTER LATE THAN NEVER

THE OTHER SIDE

Mary Shaw was ten years old when war broke out in 1939. Now, more than fifty years later, she still retained a dislike, perhaps toned down from hatred, for the race whose leader had tried to conquer the rest of the world and caused a holocaust costing millions of innocent lives. Her own family had suffered, too. Her memories of the war and the London blitz, though muted and perhaps distorted by time, were still vivid and real to her.
Her parents and her sister had survived the six years, but at considerable cost to the future health of her mother who, she now realised, had made tremendous sacrifices in order to keep the rest of them as well fed as possible. Her father, barely within military age, had not been in a reserved occupation and in any case had been graded unfit for service. That, however, did not stop him from doing what he regarded as his duty to his country. And his standards in that respect were of the highest. Despite his wife's care he had not lived to see the retirement to which he had so looked forward; mother had followed him without a long delay. Two uncles had been killed in action, one of them lost in the dreadful, unbelievable explosion which obliterated the battle-cruiser "Hood". Their families had struggled on and survived, but Mary knew for a fact that her cousins still carried within them the scars of this untimely deprivation.

Mary herself had seen out the war without evacuation from the village where she had been born, some twelve miles out of London. This was the period of which her memories were most poignant and yet at the same time dreamlike. She could still cast her mind back to small, often trivial incidents which for some reason had registered and stuck. The hot summer of the Battle of Britain, when the sky was black with German bomber formations which seemed at times almost to stand still in the sky while the ragged puffs of exploding anti-aircraft shells decorated the background as a small child wielding its first paintbrush might have done on a sheet of blue paper. The shelter in the back garden, with its simple, functional design - a brick-built rectangular box with a foot-thick concrete roof, an interior blast wall at the entrance and an emergency exit consisting of a hole in the wall filled with four huge square concrete blocks which one was supposed to be able to push out in emergency. The specification had said that the shelter was safe against almost anything bar a direct hit, but Mary remembered no reported proof of testing. Naturally none was available, and if an actual incident had disproved the claim, the propaganda machine would never have allowed the news to leak out. At least the shelter was much more comfortable than the damp, cramped conditions of one of the corrugated iron, earth covered Andersons, and after the war the girls had been allowed to make it into a den.

While the air-raids were in progress it was dangerous to move about in the open, even when wearing a tin-hat. Mary had collected pieces of shrapnel ten inches long and weighing over a pound, and these could often be found in considerable quantity. Incendiary bombs caused many roof fires, which were fought with the aid of teams of fire-watchers and myriads of stirrup-pumps, which worked by having the suction tube immersed in a bucket of water while the operator's foot held steady the outside supporting strut. The pump handle was shaped like a stirrup and a simple up and down movement of the plunger produced a stream of water through a pipe and nozzle. Mary had never seen one used in earnest, but looking back she rather imagined that the smallness of the pipe and the capacity of one ordinary bucket might not be sufficient to produce startling results. But it all helped to create an impression of preparedness, and actually doing something was always good for the nerves. Besides, a great many incendiary bombs failed to ignite, though these probably gained in efficacy by causing accidents to the people who, despite warnings, gathered them up as souvenirs.

Mary's father, having worked in the daytime, spent most of his nights at the Air-Raid Wardens' post at the end of the road, wearing dark, warm clothing, a whistle, an ARP armband and a tin-hat. There was a huge public shelter near the post, in which the family had spent uncomfortable nights before their own shelter had been built. Mary sometimes wondered what it must have been like to sleep against the tiled wall of an Underground station, as so many inner Londoners did. The warden's job produced several amusing stories, which father passed on to mother, with strict instructions to avoid repeating them. To do so would, in his view, have been committing the treasonable offence of 'Careless Talk', about which the population was constantly warned by huge, ever-changing posters.

Perhaps the strangest of the stories had occurred shortly after the enemy began using against the civilian population the same magnetic mines with which they were attacking the merchant marine upon whose courage and dedication in bringing in supplies the survival of the nation depended. Foiled in part by measures taken at sea to combat this particular menace, the Germans took to dropping the huge engines of destruction by parachute over England. There was no possible chance of aiming for any special target, so this action may in the history of the war be the first attempt to terrorise the country into submission - an attempt which failed because of the obstinacy and single-mindedness of the ordinary people who during the six years of conflict fought their own battles on the Home Front. The parachutes on which the mines came down were of a green-coloured silky fabric and came in handy for all sorts of uses if they survived the explosion of the mine. It happened quite frequently that a mine failed to explode, and one such drop took place in a field some half-a-mile from the ARP post. It was (according to legend) discovered by a farm labourer on his way to work in the early light who at first took the dim shape on the ground for a cow and kicked it to make it get up. On perceiving his error, the labourer was reputed to have broken the world record for the standing start 880 yard dash, arriving at the post breathless and goggle-eyed and scarcely able to tell his tale. The local police inspector, who happened to be there at the time, took charge. "I shall strip off," he said, "and wrap myself in a blanket. We can't afford to have the wretched thing set off by one of my buttons, can we?" He left the post feeling much less brave than his calm exterior indicated, but within a few yards was overtaken by a shout from behind him - "Hey, Fred! What about your tin helmet? " Apparently the mine was later exploded by controlled detonation.

As the war progressed, new and more fiendish weapons were devised to try and break the morale of the British people. First came the V 1, also known as flying bomb or doodlebug. This incorporated one of the first jet engines used in aircraft propulsion, for the bomb was a simple pilotless plane, packed full of explosives and launched from a ramp somewhere on the opposite coast of the North Sea. When the approximately-judged fuel supply ran out and the sinister, unmistakeable sound of the jet engine ceased, the plane fell to earth and exploded on impact. It was said that if it had gone past you before the engine stopped, you were safe, but even then one did not know whether the fall would take the form of a near-vertical drop or a shallow glide. Whichever happened, people and property at the point of impact became an extremely bad insurance risk. The V 1 was soon followed by the V 2, an even more technologically advanced machine. In fact it was the prototype of all future space-rockets, and its trajectory took it high, sometimes above the atmosphere, whence it hurtled downwards to earth and, unlike many of the doodlebugs whose blastwave did a lot of extra damage, created a large crater and an area of desolation around it. Mary remembered a rare example of a V 2 exploding on re-entry to the atmosphere. She was playing in a field across the road from her home when a tremendous bang made her look up to see a huge hoop of metal cartwheeling down from the sky.

But the terrorisation attempt fizzled out after the opening of the second front in Normandy, and the entire situation changed for the people of the Home

Counties. The end of the war came more quickly than might have been expected only two years before, and with it the trial and execution of many of the German war leaders and others over whose crimes against humanity a veil had often to be drawn. To the hundreds of thousands of people who had suffered loss, the word 'German' assumed a new and sinister meaning and the memories rankled, turning often to hatred. Life resumed, but there was much of it that was never the same again.

Mary left school, trained as a typist and rose eventually to be in charge of a typing pool in a City of London office. Every year she went abroad for a holiday, but never to Germany until the occasion when she was seduced by a package deal which seemd too cheap too ignore. For a relatively small sum, she spent a week on an English boat on a cruise up the Rhine. The coach left from Tower Hill, carrying with it food supplies for the whole week. The crew and staff were all English, and only the many differences in the landscape reminded the party that they were not still in England. Despite her geographical location, Mary enjoyed the holiday. She had no real contact with German people, but she had the chance to see the great arterial river of Germany as it flowed through magnificent, un-English scenery. Fairy-tale castles on steep mini-mountains; riverside towns and villages built in a style of domestic architecture which was new to her; the peaceful and yet awe-inspiring atmosphere of Beethoven's house in Bonn. On one sunny day the party ascended in a ski-lift to the View of The Seven Lakes - actually seven apparently unconnected stretches of the river as it wound its way through the overbearing hills of the Rhineland All these things came as a surprise - not that she had travelled with any preconceived expectations. But it was the huge twin spires of Cologne Cathedral and the fact that they and the main building were still standing which made a major impact, followed by a secondary jolt at the stark towers of the bridge at Remagen. The massive fortress of Coblenz was almost an anti-climax.
That year was one of drought, and the boat could not get upriver past the Lorelei Rock. The last couple of days were done by coach, but Mary was not interested in the tourist trap of Rudesheim, for all its importance in the world of wine. When she returned home she had no particular wish to repeat the trip, and her steadfast view of the German people had not changed.

Within a few years, Mary retired on a decent pension from her employers, and was still able to take holidays, this time off season and often cheaper than before. On one of these she was persuaded by a friend to visit the region to the north of Luxembourg, just inside the German border, the deciding factor being the promise of excellent walking country. They booked to stay for ten days in a small private hotel in a little town in the northen part of the Eifel region - a country of hills, trees and rivers, sparsely populated and containing no really large towns.

From the start, Mary was captivated by the countryside and by the early buildings in the tiny walled towns, with their architecture so colourful and different. The two women walked and took coach trips to see the Ruritanian grandeur of Luxembourg, the Roman heritage of Trier, the wine-growing region of the Ahr Valley, whose small production is all swallowed by local demand, and an assortment of tourist towns with large castles, where houses clung to the hillsides rising from the inevitable bridge and marketplace in the town centre. Above all, for the first time, Mary spoke to ordinary German people. That they were ready to speak to her was no surprise; they were, after all, in the tourist business. But that she found herself able to speak to them without the fierce resentment which she had always felt towards their nation came as a bewildering state of affairs. It also surprised her that she was able to remember so much of her schoolgirl German - not that it mattered, for most people, especially the younger ones, spoke quite good English.

Then, on the day before she was due to return home, she fell in the street and knew no more until she awoke in hospital. Tests had already indicated that she had suffered a minor heart-warning, but the doctor, in his impeccable English, advised her not to travel home for another week and called into the room the owner of the hotel where she had been staying, who also spoke her language, and whom she had hitherto come across only as one might vaguely be aware of a silent workman who oils the wheels of a vehicle or fixes a dripping tap. His name, it turned out, was Dieter. "Madame", he said to her, "your doctor tells me that you should not yet travel to England. Please be my guest until you feel well for your journey. I have only six rooms but some are not taken".

Mary was nonplussed. This was a totally unexpected development, with which one may not have met in similar circumstances in most English hotels.

"Thankyou," she replied, "I should like to stay, but I must of course pay for the extra time". "That is good", answered Dieter, with a wide smile." But you shall not pay. Instead you shall talk to me and make right the things which I do not say properly". Mary protested, without avail, but it was finally agreed that she would be allowed to pay at a special reduced rate. On the following day she was back in the hotel.

At most mealtimes, and for coffee in the morning, Dieter sat with Mary Shaw at her table. It was he who first broached the subject which had started again to simmer in her mind - this man, so charming, polite and utterly correct in his behaviour, was an enemy, one of the race which had tried to destroy her native land. They had already agreed, however, to use christian names rather than the clumsy formal alternative. "Mary," said Dieter over coffee, " I think that you are not sure that you like me. If this is because I am a German and my country was fighting your country forty years ago, I would please like to explain that at first we in Germany thought that we hated the English. We are still not an old country, like England and France. One hundred fifty years ago we were still many small countries which made war between each other. Perhaps it was that our German fathers and grandfathers were very ..." he fumbled for a word.......
"proud to be a country and wished very much to be a great country in the world. Kaiser Wilhelm was a man with a bad arm and was ashamed, so that he would listen to the generals who said that he must make this new Germany like England and France."

"So Germany did not make peace in the year of 1914, but went to war to show to the other countries that Germany was not small and weak. But in this first terrible war, when many millions of young men were dead, Germany could not have the food and the iron and other things which it needed to make war. For this we Germans were beaten and your country and France did things to make it that Germany would not again try to be great, and for many years there was hunger and sickness and trouble for our people."

" But then came this man called Adolf Hitler, and he gave us back the hope that Germany could be great again. So we followed him, but too late we saw that his dream for the great Germany was not good because it would mean war again, and this we did not want. But at that time Hitler was already the Fuehrer and his policemen were everywhere, so that we did not know what to do to stop him. I was a school teacher, and my father also. The first time that I saw my father weep was when the policemen came to him and told him that he must join the Party and teach the children new things which he did not believe, or else he would be sent away and his children would become hungry."

"Then the war came and we were told that France was ours and England would soon be ours also. But England would not be beaten, and Russia stepped back and back so that the snow and the burnt land sent back our army with no more heart to fight. And our so-wonderful Luftwaffe did not destroy the English airforce, so that the English bombers came at night to drop bombs on our railways and factories, and later the American bombers came also in the day. Josef Goebbels told us that England was beaten and that London was burnt down, but this was not true. Your Westminster Abbey and St Paul's Cathedral were not destroyed like the cathedral at Coventry. Our great Cathedral at Koln still stands also. But to some of us the burning of Dresden and many other of our towns seemed to be words from the bible, a book which we had been told to forget - ' Vengeance is mine, I will repay; an eye for an eye, a tooth for a tooth. ' And the God of the bible had looked after his own things, for so many churches were not bombed to the ground."

" When I was 16 years old I was taken to be in the army of the Fatherland, which I knew was not the land of my father. Soon the Russians began to push forward into Germany from the East, and the English and Americans came to the Rhine from the West. My regiment became soon only a company, and we marched without hope back towards Germany. We knew that the Russian soldiers were only a few kilometres away when we came to a river, and on the other side were the Americans. We knew, all of us, that if the Russians took us we would not see our homes again. Because I could speak in English my friends asked me to go across the bridge and ask the American soldiers if they would make us prisoners. The American major looked at me, only a boy in rags, and said to me words which I shall not ever forget - "Son, I shouldn't do it , but what the hell!, send your buddies across".

" So we all came safe home, and I married my wife who is now with God, and we lived at first with her mother who had come out of Berlin through the Russian army, dressed as a nun".

Dieter stopped speaking and gazed into space through a film of tears. Then he continued:- " Please, Mary, I ask you to think again that the German people are not your enemies. They know something which you English will never know, and that is the feeling to be defeated and to have their country torn apart and occupied by soldiers of other countries. They want only peace, and they know also that their leaders have brought great sorrow and death on many millions of people who did not harm them. The German people will try to forget but will always carry with them that shame for what their fathers were made to do." He rose from the table and walked slowly and sadly into his office.

That evening there was a festival in the town. There was an English jazz band and dancing and beer and singing and laughing and lights. Mary and Dieter sat at a table near the bridge under which flowed the placid river, tonight shimmering like a rainbow of reflected light. She was watching the band, whose leader played the trumpet and at the same time coordinated both the programme and the format of each tune. He was good, she thought. Dieter was watching Mary. During a lull in the general hubbub, he asked " Mary, have you thought more about our talk this morning?" Mary's gaze moved from the kind, compassionate eyes down to the gnarled hand lying at ease on the table. She rested her small, blue-veined fingers lightly on the large brown ones. "Dieter", she asked quietly, " may I stay with you, for the rest of ever?" The German smiled. "But of course," he replied, and gestured towards the band, where the leader had just embarked on a solo, clear, concise and commanding. "We have made a bridge, you and I, over a deep river. And did not your John Bunyan write, of his pilgrim, ' So he passed over, and all the trumpets sounded for him on the other side?' "

LEARNER

"Driver halt! Handbrake on! Into neutral! Into first! Up to second! Up to third! Down to second! Down to first! Driver forward! Get your foot on that accelerator, don't just tickle it. You're not fondling your first woman! " Trooper Jones, of the 74th Training Regiment, Royal Armoured Corps, was learning to drive. The war was not long over and grizzled veterans of the desert, Italy and Normandy, like the corporal beside him, were now engaged in instructing the youths who had just missed the conflict but were still being called into the citizens' army. A group of 15cwt Morris trucks was wheeling up and down a vast, disused airfield runway, in an uncannily prescient representation of the Ballet of the Hippopotami soon to be portrayed by Walt Disney in the film "Fantasia".

The instructors, mostly corporals or lance-corporals, were by now well used to the cross-section of humanity with which they were confronted every nine weeks, and had learnt to adapt their lessons according to the particular individual on the receiving end. They were not paid by results, but reasonable success tended to count when it came to the little things like an extra 48-hour pass or swapping guard duty if they had special business in the bright lights of the Camp Centre.

The driving school also attempted to inculcate upon the minds of students and shop assistants, bank clerks and bakers who had never before looked under the bonnet of a motor vehicle a rudimentary idea as to the workings of the internal combustion engine. This was more difficult, but the entire school was under the tutelage of a newly-promoted staff-sergeant whose personal capabilities were beyond question and whose methods of instruction were well-suited to the task in hand. A judicious mixture of discipline, tolerance, understanding, mastery of the subject, fairness and sarcasm seemed to be working wonders. The staff sergeant had the figure to match - six feet in height, a back as straight as a ramrod, and a physical presence backed up by a tongue as quick as a striking snake and as sharp as a dozen brand-new razor-blades. He had driven a train full of wounded the length of Greece, just catching the last naval vessel out to Egypt. Later captured by the Germans on one of the periodic pendulum swings of the North African desert campaign, he had escaped during transit in Italy and spent several months on the run in the Appenines, hiding by day in the secluded hills and emerging by night to be fed at one of the near-hovels which were home to peasants who had no stomach for the war, but a respect for their fellow-humans. A typical meal would see a vast lump of dough rolled out upon a wooden table and topped with some of the contents of a constantly-steaming cauldron full of animal offal, gut and sinew. At least it kept him alive, though it did his digestion a considerable amount of no good.

Inevitably he was recaptured, and legend had it that his treatment at the hands of his captors went way beyond the bounds of the Geneva Convention. His back, it was said , was still scarred by the marks of the whip which had been . administered 'pour encourager les autres'.

Had the Germans but realised it, they should have been well content to have him in their hands rather than facing them on the battlefield, where his exploits had also been the subject of legends, such as the assertion (not by him) that he had been a member of the crew of the only tank in history to have sunk a submarine. The archetypal soldier, he now applied to his present job in hand the same diligence and energy which he had shown in the field. Unsurprisingly he was revered in turn by each batch of recruits who came under his charge, and many a reluctant conscript was encouraged by his example to treat his army service much more seriously than might otherwise have been the case.

Once the learner-drivers had proved their ability to control a vehicle on command, the lessons widened into practical experience of driving on the roads and reacting to whatever situations arose. To this end, an occasional student would be singled out to spend a couple of hours on a long summer evening on the moorland and coast roads of North Yorkshire. It was not unknown for unscheduled stops to take place, to buy food or even to admire the scenery. On one such trip, "Staff" (as in accordance with general practice the Staff-Sergeant was familiarly referred to) was instructing a pupil who, in his view, was likely to be a bit of a problem. The trooper in question had been left under no illusion as to his status in this respect. "You will pass this course", Staff had told him in forcible terms, "or I shall have your guts for garters and your balls for earrings." The trooper, who was a typical example of a high IQ allied to a shortage of commonsense and a total ineptitude where things mechanical were concerned, was suitably impressed, even motivated to do everything possible to please this superior being who now sat beside him.

The drive proceeded well enough at first. There was little traffic on the roads, and the trooper found it relatively easy to follow the constant instructions to change gear, change direction, or come to a halt. In other words he proved capable of obeying run-of-the-mill and explicit orders. A problem arose when he was confronted with a three-point turn to be performed on a somewhat narrow road, and only managed it by dint of taking first his front and then his rear wheels to within an inch of the two-feet deep ditches lining the road and, in fact, accounting for the choice of that particular spot. The staff-sergeant betrayed no sign of emotion or panic, but his language became colourful and a great deal more expressive, and his scathing sarcasm caused the unfortunate trooper to lose what nerve he still possessed. He stopped, and faced his instructor. "It's no good, Staff", he said. "I can't seem to get it right. I know what to do but my hands and feet don't work quickly enough." "I know that, you miserable man", said Staff. "And what are you going to do about it?" The trooper looked even more despondent. "Try again, I suppose, Staff," he replied. A hint of compassion flickered momentarily in the staff-sergeant's eyes, though he took good care that his pupil didn't notice it. "Good," he said . "First off, try that turn again -SLOWLY!" Very gingerly the truck edged round, stopped a foot from the ditch, reversed equally slowly and once more stopped with plenty of room to spare. The next forward movement took the vehicle to the side of the road ready to proceed in the opposite direction to that in which it had previously been heading. "Good," said Staff. "Now do it again." And the trooper did so, a lot less hesitantly.

"Right, head for home now, and you're on your own. You're the driver, you're in control, and I'm just a passenger. Driver, forward!" The truck moved off and proceeded down the road at a steady thirty miles per hour. Until a rabbit shot out of the roadside grass right in front of it. There was a startled shout, a squeal of brakes and a crackling of branches as the vehicle buried its front bumper in the hedge. The staff-sergeant remained calm. " So why did you do that, " he enquired in a moderated tone". The trooper, still shaking with fright, considered the question. "I suppose because I panicked," he said. "You panicked in bloody spades, boy", said Staff. "The rule for you drivers is NEVER swerve for a small animal. You may be carrying fuel, explosives, or personnel and it is your job to get them safely to wherever you are going, and to hell with dogs, cats, rabbits, penguins and such. You only take evasive action if you see a human being or an animal larger than a sheep, which will not be often because cows and horses are usually safely in fields and giraffes and rhinoceri are not frequently met with in North Yorkshire. Understood, you bag of jelly, you?" The driver stopped shaking. "Yes, Staff", he said, gratefully.

"Right. Driver forward, left at the next main road AFTER STOPPING, and watch the traffic." The truck continued fairly steadily on its way. Practice on the airfield had eradicated most signs of the disorder known as 'kangaroo petrol', though there had been a slight recurrence of this after the three-point turns. Tactfully the staff-sergeant had refrained from comment.

Some twenty miles had been covered, more or less in satisfied silence, when the sound of a slight groan broke through the driver's concentration. He glanced at his instructor and saw that his head was lolling back, his face was pale and sweating and his eyes tending to roll uncontrollably. He checked his mirror and stopped beside the road. There were no houses in sight. "For God's sake, Staff", he said, "What's the matter?" The staff-sergeant managed to raise his head a little. "Probably a touch of malaria or something, "he gasped. "Feel in my top pocket and you'll find some tablets. Give me one and get me my water-bottle." The trooper did as he was told, and the instructor managed to swallow the tablet, which seemed quickly to ease his symptoms. "What now, Staff", asked the driver, anxiously."Shall I try and find a doctor?" "No, lad", was the reply. "These tablets usually work OK, but I need to get back to bed pronto. Can you do it without me?" The trooper gulped and turned pale. "I-I- d-d-on't know, Staff. I'll try" "Good man," said Staff, " Can you find the way". "I think so," came the reply. "It's mostly main road, isn't it? " The staff-sergeant nodded, a trifle feebly, and laid his head back again "Driver forward, then" he murmured.

Forty-five minutes later, as the light was just beginning to fade, the truck pulled up in front of the guard-room and a white-faced and weary trooper got out. It had been main road all the way, but some of it had been through towns and there had been a lot more traffic than he had hoped for. He went into the building, and spoke to the guard-commander. Within a minute or two the M.O. was on the spot. "Not again, Staff", he said. "Sorry, Doc," was the answer. "Just get me to bed and I'll be alright tomorrow." The staff-sergeant turned to the driver. "Get that vehicle away", he said sharply, " and report to my office at 8.30 in the morning!" The trooper scuttled off without even looking back and, having handed the truck-keys into the orderly sergeant, went wearily to bed.

Next morning the driver knocked gingerly on the door of the staff-sergeant's office. A growled "Come in" answered him, and he entered. "Attention, boy" snapped Staff; then "At ease!". He looked at the recruit critically. "So they decided that you should be a driver!", he said. " I've eaten better men than you before breakfast. As for passing your test, if last night's exhibition of three-point-turns and rabbit hunting is anything to go by, you'll fail before you're even out of the gate." The trooper hung his head and shuffled his feet. "Keep still, man" said the instructor. "You're supposed to be a soldier, not a damned jack-in-the-box! Do you think it's worth wasting the country's money carrying on trying to teach you to drive? " "No, Staff", came the sheepish answer. "You're damned right, boy. I'll not recommend you for another test, that's for sure." The trooper was nearly breaking down with shame, by now. "No more tests for you, " continued the staff-sergeant. He reached into his desk drawer, produced a piece of paper and handed it to the crestfallen figure in front of him. "Do you know what this is?" "No staff," almost whimpered the lad. "It's your pass certificate, boy. Take it. You did damned well last night, under emergency conditions. You'll make a good soldier yet. And thankyou.   March Out!"

And so another recruit turned the first corner on the way to being a trained soldier, and like many others before him he felt that if so ordered he would follow his staff-sergeant through hell and high water, no matter what the cost.

16

OVER THE RAINBOW

A little man sat on my window-sill; a thickset dwarf, short and wide
with arms outstretched on either side; motionless, silent, crouched and
grim, silhouetted through curtains dim, brooding he sat on my
window-sill.
I shuddered and hid my frightened head, for I feared his squat and
shapeless form blotting the moonlight like clouds in a storm.
He suddenly knocked on the window-pane, jerking, sidling and tapping
again, but rose at last with a hollow howl, and I feared no more.
My dwarf was an owl, a night-flying owl on my window-sill.

You all know the problems we children have with grown-ups. They're always
getting some things wrong and worrying about other things which might never
happen but would be quite alright if they did. Take rainbows, for instance.
Grown-ups will tell you that a rainbow is nothing more than sunlight seen
through tiny droplets of water. They will go on about prisoms and the spectrium
and the way light gets bent and changes colour. That's all back to front. It has to
be. Everybody knows about Joseph's coat of many colours - all the colours of
the rainbow. If a rainbow has all those colours in the first place, how can bent
light or prisoms or spectriums have anything to do with it.

Mind you, do you know what a rainbow really is? Because I'm not sure myself.
You hear all sorts of stories. Like it's a bridge for the angels to cross from one
side of the sky to the other. It can't be that; it would be far too dangerous
without railings to stop the poor angels from falling off. Then there's the idea
that it's a road for poor dead babies to walk to heaven on. Can't be that either,
because most of them can't walk and even if they could, when they got to the
other end they'd just be back on the ground again. It's got seven different
colours, a rainbow has. Did you know that? Purple, two sorts of blue, green,
yellow, orange and red. They reckon that the rainbow is a very old sort of thing
and was hidden in the sky when Old Man Noah built his houseboat to save his
family and all the animals from the big flood. They even say that it was used for
a flag to tell Noah that it was safe to get out of the boat. And I did hear once that
if you went out into the sky and looked at the world you could see that it's round,
and the rainbow, which looks like an upside-down bowl from the ground, is
actually a right-way-up bowl to catch all the water that drips off the sea when the
waves splash on the rocks.

One of the stories is about the Irish fairies who love to steal other people's gold and hide it in pots at the bottom of a rainbow. Personally I don't believe that one. I should have thought that anyoner clever enough to be a fairy wouldn't want to hide gold when he could spend it on toys and sweets and ice creams and things. Somebody else once told me that there was a sort of goddess called Iris, and she used to run messages and errands for the other gods and goddesses and she used the rainbow to get quickly from the sky where the gods all lived down to each side of the world. I've never met anyone called Iris, but the story might be right because there's a sort of flower that looks like a tall lady, and its name is Iris and its a sort of purple colour, which is one of the colours of the rainbow. And I could believe about Iris hiding her money that she got for running messages, in some place she could pick it up from on her way home.

I still think that a rainbow is like a fence between the world we live in and fairyland. "Over the Rainbow" is what some people call Fairyland, so that idea makes sense. And let me tell you I have been to Fairyland so I know what I'm talking about alright.

When did I go? Last year, if you really want to know, when my brother Billy was in bed with the measles and they sent me to stay with my great-aunt Clara till he got better. She took me. Of course she's a witch really, and frightfully clever but I bet her she couldn't make her broom-stick fly, and she couldn't, so she owed me a forfeit and I said you've got to take me to Fairyland, so she had to. I remember when I was staying with her once and I woke up in the night and there was an elf-man or a dwarf or something sitting on the window-sill at the end of my bed, so I ducked under the bedclothes. How did great-aunt Clara know he was there if she wasn't flying around outside, herself? But she did, and came in and uncovered me and twitched her fingers at him and he flew away. She told me it was only an owl, but I knew different.

Great-aunt Clara's cat is pretty clever too, though it acts stupid to hide how clever it really is. I know it's real name is Grimalkin, or something like that, but it pretends it isn't and will only come if you call it Tibby. I tried once to make it jump off the kitchen table and do a somersault, but all it did was roll on its back and wave its legs in the air and want me to tickle its tummy. I bet it can fly too if it wants to. And Great-aunt Clara has some friends who look like witches, too, and they all come round and drink tea, and ask the poor old vicar to come so as they can laugh at him. And I wouldn't be surprised if they put frogs in his sandwiches and beetlejuice in his tea.

I know that great-aunt Clara knows I believe in fairies, because she showed me how to see some of them. "They're very shy," she said, " and very careful not to be seen, but if you shut your eyes tight and press your hands over them you'll see a blue sky and if you look carefully you'll find whole crowds of fairies flying across the sky, swooping and diving. They look just like tiny soap-bubbles, but that's only to stop people seeing what they really look like."

Anyway, to get back to Fairyland, after I won my bet with great-aunt Clara about making her broom-stick fly she had to take me, and she did, the next day. We went off in the morning on a train, and then an underground train and then a bus, and then we walked a bit and came to these big gates with wire on the top. So we went in and there was a sort of little window in the wall of a shed and there was a lady behind it. I knew she was a witch too, as soon as great-aunt Clara winked at her and said "Two tickets to Fairyland, please" and the lady winked back. I've noticed this with a lot of great-aunt Clara's friends. There's an awful lot of nodding and winking and suchlike goes on between them. It must be a sort of witches' secret language.

Anyway, we went on through another gate, and there was Fairyland. Great-aunt Clara explained about how the fairies let special people in to see their country but the people had to pay the fairies money and the fairies used it to build more houses and paint the old ones in new bright colours and such. And they had a rule that while the people were about the fairies themselves mustn't move or speak at all or the whole land would be made invisible and the people would all ask for their money back.

It wasn't a very big place, but then the fairies aren't very big either. I could see some of them keeping quiet and still inside their houses. They had made special paths for full-size people to walk on, all round Fairyland among the little houses and roads and fields with small animals in. They had little shops and churches and even railway-stations, because there were loads of little trains always rattling around under bridges and through tunnels and sometimes stopping at the stations. Of course no fairies got on or off, because they weren't allowed to move about, but I bet they were always travelling around from one part of Fairyland to another when the people weren't there. We stayed for ages and I went right round Fairyland three times and looked at every house and every church and every shop and every farm, and watched every train that went by and tried to count the fairies I could see in their houses. I gave it up in the end because I'm sure they kept moving about to stop me counting them.

When I told great-aunt Clara that I was getting hungry she gave me a chocolate bar to "keep me going", she said, and we went outside and said good bye to the witch behind the little window, and she winked at great-aunt Clara and great-aunt Clara winked back at her. I bet they'd be cross if they knew I'd seen them winking. Then we went and had something to eat in a place with high chairs to sit on and a sort of long high table, and great-aunt Clara had an egg on toast and I had chicken nuggets and chips and tomato sauce and ginger beer for a treat. Then we went home, on the bus and the underground train and the ordinary train. Of course there weren't any fairies on these, but lots of people, and I asked great-aunt Clara how many people went to Fairyland. "Lots and lots", she said, "lots of children and lots of grown-ups too." I didn't say it to her, but I thought there must be millions of grown-ups who believe in fairies, else there wouldn't be so many of them keep going to Fairyland. So perhaps grown-ups aren't so bad after all.

OLD YEAR - NEW YEAR

Henry stood alone on the balcony, watching the sea as it swelled, swayed, rippled and heaved gently in the moonlight, with almost the same hypnotic effect as a cobra or a belly-dancer. Some twenty yards away, the edge of a low cliff hid the actual point where the waves dissolved on the sand, but he could hear their regular thump and sigh as if he were listening through a stethoscope to the slow, massive breathing of some giant organism.
It was twenty minutes before midnight in the Algarve, and it was New Year's Eve. Henry always had problems coping with time changes, but he assumed that in England the twelve deep chimes of Big Ben had already set off the usual mass hysteria in Trafalgar Square and the fountains were waiting with calm resignation for the standard intrusion of over-excited human bodies. They were not worried, of course. They always had the last laugh as the bodies rapidly regained sensibility and retired with chilled bones and chattering teeth but believing themselves to be the heroes of the hour.

But on the balcony the night was soft and liquid, filled with warmth and fragrance and the drone of cicadas punctuating the all-pervading music of the sea. On the cliffs and the beach below, crowds were gathering for their own celebrations. Here on the Algarve the people and the customs were refreshingly strange. The people were relaxed, sometimes to the point of lethargy. Their broad shoulders grew bowed as they aged; perhaps this was a by-product of the constant shrugging which characterised the "manana" syndrome, but it could also have resulted from the centuries of hot sun which must have thinned their blood. Certainly the locals tended to wear fur coats while the visitors were too hot in shorts.

Nonetheless, Henry liked them for their tolerance, courtesy and generally happy outlook on life. They did not always have much incentive to be thus. Traditionally the Algarve was a region of fishermen who for many years had spent half their lives three thousand years away on the Grand Banks, while their wives kept up their meagre houses and looked after the children, invariably wearing black in readiness for the non-return of their menfolk. Henry remembered Spencer Tracy's portrayal of Manoel in the film "Captain's Courageous". Thinking about it, he was impressed by the accuracy of the casting, for the squat, thickset Tracy was very much like the local men.

Now of course, the fishing had dwindled to the few curly-prowed wooden boats with outboard engines which on every available small beach could be seen during the day drawn up beyond the tidemark amid a tangle of nets and rubbish, and during the night in the shape of twinkling lights a mile out to sea. The men seemed to do little else, but stood on street corners smoking and talking and more often than not drinking medronho, the local schnapps made from the fruit of the arbutus trees which grew wild in the foothills of the Serra. It was these mini-mountains, in a long line parallel to and some twenty-five miles from the coast, which proteced the region from the northern weather and gave the Algarve its own, sunny mini-climate. Henry had been to a medronho still, with its heaps of rotting fruit and its single large copper vessel from which dripped the clear distilled liquid. In its pure form this was very much an acquired taste and went down more easily if tossed back like vodka, not touching the sides. But, ever with an eye to business, the local distillers rapidly diverted some of their produce to a system which delayed bottling long enough for the liquid to enjoy a sojourn in oak casks and thus take on a certain colour and mellowness which made it more palatable to visiting tastebuds and at the same time more profitable to producers' pockets.

Henry had tried both sorts and disliked neither. He would take home a bottle of the aged stuff to impress and perhaps surprise his friends, but enjoyed most of all an Algarve coffee - strong, sweet and black and with a good lacing of the white, rough medronho. The sweetness was another Algarvian trait, for the inhabitants had an inordinate love of confectionery of all types and shops for its sale were spread throughout the entire hundred-mile length and thirty-mile breadth of the region. From the wide river to the east and the endless ocean to the west, except of course for the many desolate areas of scrubby or tree-covered hills, one was never far from sweetness.

Henry and his wife had floated up the Guadiana river between Portugal and Spain, disembarking at the turning point of the trip to enjoy a lunch of sardines and salad, washed down with an unlimited supply of the little-appreciated but remarkably good local wine. And on another day they had visited the lighthouse on Cape St. Vincent and wandered over the cliff-site of Henry's Navigator-namesake's school for explorers, in which could still be seen his huge compass-dial set out in rock and stone on the ground beneath the great walls of the fortress. From the cliffs one could watch the local fishermen, who fearlessly climbed down to precarious vantage points two hundred feet above the sea and rocks below and fished unconcernedly with rod and line. Every year one or more of them fell to his death, but the survivors simply gave the usual shrug of the shoulders and explained that as they took their living from the sea, so must the sea expect payment. "The ocean gives and the ocean takes away. That is life". And this queer partnership between sea and land went on for ever as, across the bay northward to the Cape, three-mile long Atlantic rollers marched steadily, rank upon rank, to shatter on the massive face of the western rock wall of the Algarve.

The celebration of Christmas and New Year in Portugal was much different to the commercially extended and basically meaningless approach commonly found in England. On the Algarve, New Year was more important in many respects than Christmas, but neither was allowed to interfere unduly with life, work or business. This, Henry reflected, was similar to the ethos which he had found years previously in Denmark, where the watchwords seemd to be "Work hard - Play hard", and the streets of every small town would be crowded with folk enjoying themselves well after midnight, but at 8 a.m. those same people would be at their place of work with their noses to the grindstone. There was a difference, however. By no stretch of the imagination could the Danes be described as "laid back", while in the sun of the Algarve a position of relaxation was the norm.

Christmas in Portugal lasted only a day or two, with sometimes a short run-up to what was essentially a quiet, family day when lunch would be taken together at home and those people capable of walking afterwards would take the children -adults and children alike attired in their best clothes - to the nearest pastellaria and there consume many calories in the form of a huge variety of the sweet, syrupy cakes which they so liked. Then , the following day it was back to work.

On New Year's Eve, after work had finished, the streets, the restaurants and the beaches would be packed with crowds of relaxed revellers eager and willing to welcome into their celebrations the visitors, who appeared slightly mesmerised by all this unexpected activity. There would be shouting and singing, dancing and drinking, music and merriment until at midnight the turn of the year was signalled by fireworks. Henry had been struck dumb with amazement and surprise on his first acquaintance with Portuguese fireworks. There were no pretty-pretty, namby-pamby Golden Rain, Shooting Stars, Catherine Wheels or simple Sparklers. The Roman Candles and Rockets considered so extreme by many English folk were as cap-pistols compared to the projectiles launched in celebration and without apparent aggression by the Portuguese New Year revellers. As it happened, Henry had in fact seen the like before, and was strongly reminded of his boyhood during the war when the flak went up with deafening cracks on the ground, quickly answered by enormous hollow bangs in the sky, marked by spreading puffs of white, grey, yellow and brown smoke at the point where each shell burst. The homemade Portuguese artillery looked and sounded just like that, but was succeeded by the resumption of the noise of enjoyment and happiness. For some reason the whole show was reminiscent of the Chinese celebrations of the divinity of dragons and the expulsion of evils.

As the anti-aircraft fire tore the sky apart, Henry's wife joined him on the balcony, came into his arms and kissed him. "Happy New Year, darling" she whispered. And she meant it. The old year had not been particularly happy for the two of them. Henry's wife had suddenly fallen victim to the prevailing practice on the part of employers of getting rid of staff whenever this was possible cheaply and without penalty. She had less than a year before her State pension kicked in, and was not entitled to compensation of any sort. Henry was in a similar position, though by his own action. His normal robust health had been undermined by years of long hours and stress, and he had decided unilaterally to retire eighteen months early. His employers did not want him to go and spitefully made it much more difficult for him than necessary. He too had to wait for his pension. The Algarve holiday which they were now enjoying would be their last for a couple of years, for on their return home they planned to move from their top-storey flat in London's East End to a small house in a Northern town, where property prices and living generally were a lot cheaper. Apart from the cost angle, the seaside or the open country were not for them. They were city-dwellers to the core, preferring the irregular roar of traffic to the pregnant, thudding sound of silence.

Other things had marred the old year. Returning home from a weekend in the West country, they had found it difficult to open their front door. The interior of their home was a shambles, with drawers, clothing, furniture and household items strewn everywhere. Practically every piece of electrical equipment in the flat had gone, even the vacuum cleaner, and much else besides. The insurance company had been very good and settled their claim quickly and compassionately. But no amount of money could replace the sentimental value of Henry's great-grandfather's silver half-hunter watch and chain, which Henry was planning to pass on to his son, or his wife's costume jewellery received years ago as a twenty-first birthday present.
Worst of all was the trauma of knowing that personal things had been defiled by the touch of insensitive villains probably either stealing to order or to buy drugs. It was very strange, too, that the neighbours on the same floor, five storeys up,

had heard nothing, though the noise of the break-in and the ransacking must have been considerable. Then Henry had fallen ill, first with a hyperthyroid condition which fortunately had been diagnosed and treated quickly by an alert G.P., and again when he had fallen, split his head open and suffered from severe dizziness and sickness necessitating a brain scan. At least, as he liked to say, they had found that he had got one.

They would be flying home the following day, refreshed and ready to re-organise their lives in accordance with their concept of retirement. A small cosy home, close to shops and a bus route, and fitted out with essentials which hopefully would cover future sickness or disabilities. Space for a small library and equipment for other hobbies such as music. The facility to indulge Henry's fancy for putting something back into the community which in general terms had supported him from birth to retirement. The new home was in a sadly-decaying inner city area in which there was plenty of scope for community work, especially regeneration. Henry's wife liked the idea of doing something which as a girl she had never been allowed to do - tap-dancing, - while Henry himself had at the back of his mind the possibility of going back to his schooldays and perhaps taking up literature again - maybe even trying to do a bit of writing.

They stood together on the balcony as the boisterous crowds below began to disperse. Henry's arm was round his wife and her head rested gently on his shoulder. The holiday had been restful, interesting and not too expensive. Money was not too plentiful, but money was not everything. Their health was fine, their children were doing well for themselves and had become friends as well as family, and it was worth a year of careful planning to know that with luck there were many more fruitful years ahead. "We'll make it, love", said Henry; "Happy New Year". "Yes, dear", replied his wife; "Life is good".

GAMEMASTER

Gibble passed into the entrypoint and began to reintegrate his conscious essence, automatically embedding it in the form which he always assumed for this particular Game. Concentrating on this job, he failed to notice the ingress of another entity until a voice in his just-materialised ear said "Boo!" "Lay off it, Miggle," he grunted, "it's bad enough having to come here again so soon without being spooked by the first feathered fool that happens by. Besides, our revered Boss is driving me crazy with his weird ideas to improve this cockeyed board. He should have scrapped it eons ago." "Keep your wings on," retorted Miggle. " If you don't like being chief fixer for Xoox you can always go and work for Loox."

"Don't be damned stupid," snarled the other, who now, halfway through the process of assumption, looked rather like a huge plastic puffball. "Xoox is the greatest, most successful Gamemaster in the universe. As for Loox, I wouldn't trust him with a kid's lollipop, never mind a board like this. Though why Xoox should have spent so much time and effort on this one I can't imagine. Personally I would have trashed it ten times by now." He was now completely ready, a mirror image of Miggle, making a pair of gigantic birds; this of course was all show for the benefit of the myriads of mini-pieces which made up the counters in this Game.

The pair turned towards the board exit. "Watch it", warned Miggle. "These minis are getting too blasted curious for my liking. They're practically living here now. It was much better when they couldn't stand the cold and the distance." Gibble paused, thoughtfully. " You could be right," he said; "come to think of it, there's been a sort of logical progression going on for some time. Are they beginning to suspect more than might be good for them? There was that lot who they called their idol 'Zeus', the idea of keeping animals for show in what they disrespectfully call a Zoo, and then the food essence that got marketed as OXO, just to mention three instances. It might not be coincidence, you know, that these words are a bit like 'Xoox' ". "If they are," replied Miggle, "it's entirely his own fault. I always thought he was overprogramming the little shits. And I was never sure that he was right telling us to make ourselves look like this, even if it does impress the minis. Why birds?" "That I can understand", Gibble answered, flexing his wings. "They're a superstitious lot - Xoox built that in as a safeguard - and in the basic piece-hierarchy in this Game the bird is the best. It can walk and fly, and also swim, which no other piece can do. That's quite clever, really, considering there's so much damned water in this place. And there's nothing like a bit of aerobatics over the top of a load of gawpers with cricks in their necks. Even the name they've given us shows a bit of respect." The two beings emerged from the entrypoint into a white polar waste and launched themselves into the frozen sky. "For Pete's sake go invisible," yelled Miggle. "We don't want any more rubbish about unidentified flying objects or religious fervour over a sighting of angels". "Sorry," said Gibble, "I forgot."

The ultimate beings in the universe were in reality very much as might be expected - incorporeal concentrations of sentience possessing awesome powers over the ten dimensions in which they existed. Miggle needn't have worried. So far the prowlers around the entrypoint could barely understand three-and-a-half of those ten so still had six-and-a-half to go.

The Game on which Gibble and Miggle were working was one of many thousands dotted over the illimitable, infinite space which acted as a playground for these beings - immortal, invisible and wise beyond all conception. Their recreation was The Game - a spatial equivalent of the virtual reality toys to which the minis on Gibble's board had recently aspired. The supreme beings set great store by these games, which were both their work and their play - the channel through which their energies rode the dimensions and kept up the movement necessary to prevent the universe from reverting to a total void. A few of these entities devoted their time (in the sense of a single dimension) to the evolvement and manufacture of Games, most of which were designed to be played on boards interspersed throughout "space". The boards themselves were created from the cosmic dust which itself was a phenomenon self-perpetuated from previously discarded Games. In effect, the universe was a circle, with each dimension operating on separate radii from a common centre which was both nothing and infinity. It was this circular form which gave it its permanence. The acknowledged master of the art of creating Games was an entity known as Xoox, and his most bitter competitor was Loox. Each Gamemaster employed a small staff of assistants whose job it was to supervise first the construction and then the operation of the Games. Gibble and Miggle were responsible for Xoox's most popular board, a long-running entertainment known as "Earth", which had undergone a great many revisions and refinements since its first creation.

Of this Game, Xoox's rival Loox was insanely jealous and was always attempting to bring about its failure. The word "jealous" in its universal sense implies a wish either to possess or to destroy. For the one purpose of all this great all-pervading universe was the perfection which could be achieved only by the simultaneous turning-in on its centre of each circular dimension, and this could be brought about solely by the fusion of all the entities into one all-powerful whole. This totality, needing no further purpose, would become at the same time nothing and everything. A single Game played by every possible participant would obviously facilitate that fusion.

Surprisingly, the minipieces on Earth seemed to understand this concept, which they described variously as "squaring the circle" or "revolving in ever decreasing circles, eventually disappearing up one's own rectum." Never before had any game used pieces into which so much potential power had been built. Being on the spot, Gibble was the most knowledgeable exponent of the theory behind this -apart from Xoox, of course, but Gibble was probably in a better position to detect incipient flaws in the system or to identify possible errors in the levels of decision-making allowed as compared to the quality of capability to make those decisions.

He had watched without comment the initial construction of the board for Earth, a standard and logical process slanted in this instance towards the " balance of elemental quality" theory. The first pieces had been crude, mainly because of their direct derivation from elemental sources. There had been a good deal of switching between elements until the first workable rules could be formulated. These Games took eons to evolve, and for much of that time were unplayable due to their basic instability and lack of attraction. It was not until the debris of board construction had settled down and the first massive, cumbersome and unintelligent pieces had been replaced through natural evolution that a viable concept for the Game itself could begin to be worked up into a format sophisticated enough to satisfy the tastes of the most discriminating entity. Eventually evolution had fined down the minipieces into a sort of 'Best Value' shape and thereafter the progression of the Game quickened considerably.

This Game in its current from, thought Gibble, was about as sophisticated as you could get, in fact so far advanced that it was in danger of collapsing under the weight of its own complexity. He sighed when he harked back to the strong simplicity of the early rules and their uncompromising insistence on progress based only on established certainty. The players had vied with each other to circumvent these strict rules, and nearly destroyed the Game in the process. Gibble suspected that Loox had had more than a hand in this. The minis were manipulated until they had backed into different corners from which they tried to escape by means of fighting among themselves, both individually and groupwise. The turnover of maimed and useless pieces was enormous and their replacement had been a major problem. And still the inter-mini carnage went on, becoming more and more cunning in character. Xoox had actually visited the board site - a practically unprecedented event. He had talked at length to Gibble, who had argued strongly against cutting the losses already incurred and destroying the whole thing. "Your problem", he had told Xoox, " is mainly with the players, and the only way I can see of getting round it is to increase the capabilities of the pieces. You know I have never been in favour of this, but if you want to save the Game, I can see no other way." Xoox pondered this advice. "You may be right," he said. " Can you handle it if I do something drastic - a sort of compromise?" "What do you have in mind, Boss?", asked Gibble. "I will give the little so-and-sos a bit more latitude and increased decisional parameters," replied the Gamemaster. "But I cannot afford to give that to all of them. The bad eggs will have to go. You arrange the culling and I'll promise to reprogramme what's left." "You're the Boss", shrugged Gibble, and Xoox returned to his position in infinity.

The first thing Gibble did was to take on an assistant, and so Miggle came to Earth for the first time. He was fascinated and a bit daunted, but he could see the reason for making the Game viable again. Between them they came up with a plan which combined cunning use of the elements and of the unstable nature of many of the manipulated pieces. "You draw up a shortlist of the minis worth keeping," instructed Gibble. " I'll work out a modus operandi which will satisfy the players but still achieve the objective." The Game could not be taken out of service, of course, for fear of loss of business credibility. And so, shortly afterwards , the board was refurbished by the simple process of turning water, air and fire against earth. First, however, Miggle had arranged for the survival of the best of the minipieces and of all the natural adjuncts to life to which they had become used. "This is what you have to do," he told Noah, his chosen piece-leader, " and be sure you don't leave out a single species. They've all got to survive or the whole plan won't work."

After the deluge things went a bit more smoothly for a while. Until, that is, one particular group of minis had tried to impose their ideas on other groups. Gibble strongly suspected that Loox had been behind this development, but could not prove it. One thing that followed was a huge increase in requests to play, and because of the many different approaches tried by the new players the whole situation threatened to get out of hand again. Dominant groups rose by the efforts of one player and were promptly knocked down by another. Empires were built, and empires were destroyed - not always by conquest but sometimes by sheer negligence or by too much enthusiasm on the part of the players. At least all these comings and goings held down the rate of technological change for a while.

This, however, proved to be a false directional pointer. As the board grew in usable size, and the minis multiplied with astonishing rapidity considering the wastage rate, it became obvious that there was in fact a direct relationship between periods of wide conflict and surges in the rate of technological development. It appeared that incredible leaps in invention were made in the cause of more efficient weaponry and later applied towards peaceful purposes. Materials were discovered and modified, communications between areas were improved out of all recognition, movement across the board became easier and much more rapid. But at the same time disputes between mini-groups proliferated, often over very trivial matters.

Meanwhile, the minis were constantly probing everywhere for explanations of fresh questions. Physical problems were succeeded by abstruse issues of mixed-up metaphysics, such as "how many angels can stand on the point of a needle?". "Angels" was the name given early on by the minis to Gibble and his team who, despite strict rules and great care would slip up from time to time and provide a glimpse of themselves to some stunned mini-piece, who would run demented to his fellows and preach all sorts of rubbish which had little connection with the 'angels' but was often useful for purposes such as whipping up enthusiasm for a quick war or two.

It was never clear whether it was the occasional sightings of angels or the constant proximity of birds which had set the minis off in a frantic search for a mechanism which enabled them to fly. Whichever it was, it was bad news for the future. Firstly it multiplied manifold the dreadful machinery of destruction which could be brought to bear during the ever-increasing number of conflicts. When a lull in this activity finally came, energies were diverted to extending the flight capability into the space between the Board and the countless others which were still being used or invented. At this point, Xoox began to get a bit worried. "What now?" he asked himself. "Is there a way in which I can change the rules so that players are restricted as to what they can allow their pieces to do? Do I need to have another cull? Either way I cannot push backwards the technological advances which have so far been made. If I close the whole thing down my credibility as a Gamemaster will be seriously undermined. But if these minis ever manage to reach another board, the consequences do not bear thinking about."

He sent for Gibble.

Gibble appeared in a somewhat harrassed state. Having been close to the problem, he too had done a tremendous amount of thinking about it. "If you want my advice,Boss" he said, "here it is:-   1. The players are beginning to scent some sort of unprecedented event which might make you a bit of a laughing-stock. This would not exactly upset a lot of them, so they are directing their efforts towards forcing a crisis point, when they will sit back and watch us trying to deal with it. 2. There are rumours of a group of players getting together to form a sort of hidden agenda with Loox, and we both know what that might mean. And 3, the situation on the board is escalating at an alarming rate. The minis are sending their machines farther and farther towards the boundaries of the Board Sector, and more serious are the effects which their experiments, combined with their increased uses of elemental resources for normal existence purposes, are having on the structure of the board itself.
As I see it, Boss, there are three avenues by which the problem can be tackled. 1. is through the players, but they are getting all fired up at the prospect of some unusual excitement so they are unlikely to co-operate. 2. is by our intervention and 3. is to leave it to the pieces themselves. The trouble with 3. is that the minis have an unprecedented capability of unilateral action, but I would not trust them either to realise what they are doing wrong, or, if they did realise it, to act quickly to solve the problem. They are now a long way from stupid , but at the same time they seem to have lost the capacity for straight thinking which was so strong in pieces like old Noah. Nowadays they call it "commonsense", but in fact it is far from common. Also, players recently have been tending to make moves designed to accentuate one of the worst and most dangerous of mini-characteristics. And that is greed and self-interest. I'm afraid that left to themselves the minis are bound to destroy the board sooner or later - probably sooner. It might come quickly with an explosion, or it might come slowly. I once heard one mini saying something about 'an unconscionable time a-dying,' and I think that is how 'slowly' would be. So that leaves us with option 2, which is something which we have always regarded as a last resort. Gamemaster, I believe that we have come to that point if you want to save this board - the greatest and best of all your Games. "

Xoox was silent for what seemed an eon of time. Then, "I don't want to lose it," he said. " I regard it as the most positive step ever made towards the achievement of perfection. I seem to recall on several occasions activating some sort of demonstration designed to shock the pieces into a state of awe and serious dread, which in turn has made them return to the ideals of group behaviour which they

themselves have set up. I believe that they refer to it it as "religion". Is it worth our while thinking along those lines again?"
Gibble shook his head. "Wouldn't work now, Boss," he said. "There are so many different rival groups in the religion business that it would be impossible either to mount a demonstration which would impress every one of them, or to get them to co-operate in any case. The only thing I can think of does involve the demonstration option, but in a different way and with a different objective."

"Let's have it, Gibble", said Xoox. " Something has got to be better than nothing." Gibble went on:- " Think of it like this, Boss. The pieces know that they are dicing with death, but despite multiple warnings from the few sensible ones able to make themselves heard, the majority are still firmly on the self-interest path. For instance, there is one group which knows perfectly well that they are thinning the atmosphere surrounding the board by over use of certain modern technologies. Most other groups are doing something about it, but not this one. Their leader is scared rigid of losing his comfortable position because of offending the powerful pieces who control and benefit from what they call 'business'."
" Business, on the board, is slanted entirely to the accumulation of a completely artificial commodity which the minis call 'money'. All personal belongings, assets and commodities of any kind are eventually valued in terms of money, and to many of the minis, money has become that rather more idealistic concept which I mentioned earlier - religion. They even have a board game of their own, where they compete against each other to amass the most 'wealth '. I accept that this is based on their real existence, but it makes me laugh to see fully-matured pieces squabbling over putting little model buildings on fictitious sites. Besides, who ever heard of a pyramid in Paris or a store in the middle of the Sahara."

Gibble paused before going on. "Now, money has many forms on our board, each one suited to a particular group of pieces and to the board location at which that group is situated. For movement between locations, money has to be changed into a movable form, and this is usually some sort of elemental commodity, like the yellow metal which the minis call 'gold', or small chips of carbon rock which they call 'diamonds'. Recently, too, an abstract form of portable money has been invented. This they call 'international credit', and it works by way of small electronic boxes which communicate with each other. Now, I reckon that if we can destroy all the money on the board, the pieces will start trying feverishly to replace it , and because they are not stupid will be careful about how they do it. They will soon come up with some alternative form of transferable money, but I am convinced that, at this point, they will attempt to reverse the trend to self-destruction."

"Logical thinking", said Xoox. "How do we do it?"

"Not very easily", replied Gibble. " I can't think offhand of any one action which will achieve the entire range of the objective. They have legends about the gold and diamonds, and in fact at one stage, before they knew better, they spent ages trying to turn lead into gold. So they might react in the right way if we turned all the gold into lead, and we could easily turn the diamonds into glass which they look like anyway. As for the little boxes (which they call 'computers', by the way,) that is much easier. It appears that these are vulnerable to certain diseases, which strikes me as being a bit funny for something which is descended from a long line of highly sophisticated machines. If we can simply plant a boardwide itch which causes every computer to scratch itself to death, and at the same time destroy the most important materials (like the one they call silicon) which are currently used in computer construction, it will take some time to put all this right. Then we may be able to steer them back into a consideration of commonsense.But be careful we keep Loox out of this"

Xoox meditated - not for as long as on the previous occasion. "So be it," he said. "See to it, Gibble, and call on me for any help you need. I will deal with Loox. Good luck."
"On my way, Boss, "said Gibble.

So, if your sovereigns and your wedding-rings go grey, your diamond earrings lose their sparkle and you find that the manufacture of computers suddenly comes to a grinding halt and your own PC has melted overnight into a mass of twisted plastic and metal, you will know what is happening. Take heed, because if the Gamemaster's (or rather Gibble's) plan doesn't work, you won't get another chance.

STATE OF MIND

I must have been about fourteen when I first started to visit the old man who lived in a small, neat cottage at the bottom end of our village. I was trying to earn a bit of pocket money by delivering groceries for the village store, and on my first call at the cottage it was immediately obvious why delivery was necessary. The door was answered by an elderly gentleman with a white stick, who courteously took the small bag of goods from me, insisted that he could now manage, and fumbled in his trouser pocket for the sixpence which he passed over to me with simple and unassuming grace. "Thanks, lad," he said; " I can't get about much myself nowadays."

During the next few weeks the delivery was repeated. Each time a sixpence would be offered and thanks returned, in different words which began to turn into a conversation. After a fortnight I suddenly realised that the old man was very interesting and at the same time probably lonely. I had found out that he had a cleaning lady in once a week, and I wondered how he managed alone for the rest of the time. Next time I went I handed him back his sixpence. "Please sir," I told him, " you don't need to do that every time. And if you need any help, like odd jobs and so on, I'll be glad to come." He turned his sightless eyes towards me, and returned the coin to his pocket without demur. "Lad," he said, "That's the best offer I've had in years. There's nothing I can think of needs doing at the moment, but how about you just coming to talk and keep me company for a while?" The gratitude in his voice was so obvious that it rang out like an Easter hymn in the ancient village church. "Of course, sir," I replied. And we settled for after tea on the following day.

When I arrived I found lemonade and a few biscuits on a tray, with two glasses and plates. "I expect you've had your tea", said Mr.Fairweather (I had found out what his name was), " but if you fancy a drink I'll have one with you." And so we got to talking - or at least, he did.
I learned that he was not actually what he called 'black blind', but could distinguish shapes in a good light, and that he had been an artist until his sight got too bad to carry on. He pointed to the walls of the room. Every available space contained a painting, forming a mass of colour which contrasted weirdly with the sparse and simple furnishings. "All mine", he said simply, and left it at that. We talked of his life and mine, and of what plans I might have for the future. "If I could see a bit better", he said, " I'd offer to give you drawing

lessons." I shook my head, and immediately realised that he probably couldn't see the motion. "It wouldn't be any good anyway, sir", I replied. "I'm no good at all at drawing, but I can make things". That interested him and we talked about models and carpentry for a bit, before I had to get home to do some revision for next day's lessons. "Come again soon," he said as I left; and I had every intention of doing just that. It was years before the depth of my ineptitude at art came home to me with the realisation that I could not even put two straight lines at random on a piece of paper without making it obvious that they could never harmonise in any way, but would always have the sterile quality of inalienable separateness.

Throughout my teens and my examination years I continued to visit Mr. Fairweather. He discussed with me the problems which I found in my school work, the careers for which I might like to aim, and best of all the pains of adolescence which I found difficult to raise with my parents despite our mutual family love and respect. He told me about love and its joys and its pitfalls, about society and its strengths, and how necessary it was for every person to find his or her own level in relationship to the whole. At no time did he attempt to prejudice me, but constantly emphasised the need for self-help, self-assessment and self-revelation . "A man is what he makes of himself", he would say; "But most important in that making is the individual reaction to all the exterior forces and influences which crowd in on all sides. If you make a good choice, based on instinct which has been firmly rooted in an awareness of the social concept of right and wrong and the inter-relationship between the individual and the group, you can do no more."

When I left home to complete my National Service, I avoided the embarrassment of writing, but telephoned occasionally and always visited the aging artist during my leaves. There followed another period away from home, when I went to University and returned with a good degree. Mr Fairweather was delighted and his pride rivalled that of my own father. I was delighted, too, when I obtained a post on the teaching staff of a nearby Grammar School and was able to live at home, with a bit of spare time time to resume my visits to Charles. He had already taken to referring to me as "Young" (short for young lad), but since my return from the Army he had placed our relationship on christian-name terms. "Between friends," he said, "That is only right and proper. I insist!"

It was after this time that, as he said, with my future settled we might talk more about the past. Despite my lack of manual dexterity in the field of art it had been impossible for me not to have learned from him the appreciation of it. And as he continued deeper into his own past, his achievements and his disappointments, it came home to me that he was not merely a sad shell of a once talented man, but a repository of knowledge and experience which was there on tap for someone whom he liked and trusted. In fact he was offering it freely to me. From that time our relationship progressed almost to a mystical level on which nothing was hidden and from which nothing was excluded. And from that time, too, I began to see through his own inner eyes some of the essential truths about art, beauty and life.

He knew exactly where each picture in his collection was hung, whether it was his own or a reproduction of somebody else's work; and he knew each picture as intimately as though his external eyes could see them. Using them as object lessons and illustrations he guided me through the life-years of an artist, formative, creative and now retrospective. For me the most interesting and instructive subject was the importance of Woman in the artist's mind. I was then still not only unmarried but not particularly knowledgeable about the opposite sex. Charles must have realised this, for he took great care on every possible occasion to bring it into the equations which he was propounding. His own experiences and opinions shook me to my simple core.

He had apparently never been particularly enamoured with the schools of painting and sculpture which existed before the beginning of the twentieth century and thus did not have much by way of images of them to show me. Rather surprisingly, however, he had a considerable regard for the almost photographic styles of Canaletto and David, and this was to a certain extent reflected in his own landscape work. But he took me through the intricate relationships between an artist and the women in his life, baring without hesitation his own soul in the process. He first pointed out the changes over centuries, which had gathered so much momentum that they proved impossible to stop and overran the understanding of the common man to such an extent that art appreciation became a thing for an elite society, totally scornful of anyone and anything outside its own circle. He showed me the cold classicism of the school which continued at least through to Angelica Kaufman, and contrasted it with the stony 19th century symbolism of the Pre-Raphaelites. Above all, he talked about himself and his wife and his models.

At that point it dawned on me that Charles was the ultimate sensualist - not of course in a purely sexual connotation - and seemed to have achieved a rare combination of the bodily senses with the higher intelligence of the soul. He believed that the greatest gift of mankind was that of the senses, but that it was useless without interpretation through the intellect. He had married, as artists tend to do, one of his models, and had loved her until her untimely death in a childbirth which killed also their unborn son. He had not remarried. Among his own paintings there were portaits of women, beautiful , plain, striking and nondescript. Without exception the focal point of the picture was their eyes. Charles always sought for a woman's soul in the depths of her gaze, as though he saw in it the mirror of her inner thoughts. This, at least of the six senses, was portayable on a canvas. The others were not so amenable, but although he did not say so it was obvious to me that Charles never judged except on the whole range of bodily feeling, and that he would not venture to express an opinion in paint without the benefit of a clear comprehension, though not necessarily experience, of the whole range of sensations. He believed implicitly in the existence of a sixth sense, which he equated with understanding between souls in a way which was exclusive to the communicants.

About the remaining senses he waxed lyrical, speaking of the private joys of physical love - the touch of flesh on flesh bringing the sensation of the surface smoothness of skin and the still depths of the softness beneath, with the electric currents of desire welling up from below; the smell of a woman's hair, like dry flowers in a hot summer meadow , and the scent also of everyday bodily fluids, sweat and semen and saliva, sometimes perhaps overlain by a lingering mist of a subtle and persuasive perfume applied not to deceive but to attract and bind; the taste of tongue and lips, not strong in itself but very, very personal and often identifiable with shared pleasures of food and wine; and the sounds of desire and satisfaction which between lover and beloved are so intimate and different from the craving and gratification of simple lust. All these things, Charles believed, combined to amplify and crystallise the perceptions of the sixth sense.
When I fell in love, I did not of course analyse each feeling as I experienced it, but later reflection clearly confirmed the logic of his theory.

It was natural and terribly sad for Charles to hark back to the days when he could see. But he did so entirely without embarrassment, and pointed unerringly, one by one, to paintings done in his younger days, describing the circumstances and sensations which had contributed to their composition. "Sea and Sand" was one, a seascape obviously painted somewhere on the south-west coast. Closing his eyes, he recalled an extended cycling tour during which he obtained much material for a series of such works. He had stood, he said, at the edge of a yellow cliff apparently held together by tufts of tough grass, and watched the interplay of three of the great Elements - Water, Earth and Air. The white border of the ever-moving sea swayed like the fur-trimmed tweed of a woman's skirt, and the rippled sands were cloth of gold, shadowy-black at every fold. Broken sea-walls obtruded here and there like mould on the material. Evening had fallen like a misty veil over the blue sky, until it blended with the greens and greys of the sea in a mystic bond. In all that dusky canopy, none could say where sky began or sea had end.

On another day, Charles told me, he had climbed a hill by a steep brown road, hot and dusty and welcoming every little touch of cool breeze which deigned to come near him. At the summit he had stopped to rest, and there burst on him a revelation in green and brown - the semi-circular view of the valley below him. Trees, fields and hedges, hillocks, nettles and dells - a dozen different shades of green - criss-crossed by sun-brown tracks and falling gradually to a stream half-hidden by trees. And in one meadow, beyond a pasture dotted with cotton-wool sheep, there stalked a huge stallion, his skin shining and glinting like a polished chestnut. This painting Charles had named "Symphony in Green and Brown".

The third and last in the series blazed on the wall like an explosion of red, orange and yellow. The subject was simple - just a fireplace with a hint of mantelpiece at top and sides and of rug at the bottom. The fire within raged and roared visibly, in turn dazzling, flickering and glowing. In every square inch of the painting could be discerned hints of sub-pictures - this tall yellow tongue of flame was the spire of a burning church; that one over there, more orangey-red in hue, was a fiery wizard bowing low to the viewer before vanishing into the glow of hot red embers waiting below. Faces of friends of bygone years, marching figures in reds and greys, flaming armies with flashing spears, all bound in the glorious deep beauty of red.

Charles told me of his despair when his sight was taken from him, as though a thundercloud was moving inexorably across his vision, and how for a long time he hovered between a stricken life and a dishonourable, self-induced death. Eventually, he said, the help and support of his many friends and the unstinting comfort afforded him by some of the models whom he had painted in the past had seen him through the crisis, and although he could of course no longer paint he was able to recall many of the scenes which he had enjoyed in his youth and some of the works of art which he had known and appreciated, and even to visualise new pictures from verbal descriptions.

This confirmed my impression of the reason why he had so often asked me to read to him, and I also appreciated the strength of character which had enabled him to leap across the chasm of his personal despair and to offer the benefit of his hideously expensive experience to others. I realised, too, that what Charles was saying was yet another confirmation of his theory about the alliance betwen the soul and the six senses. Neither of these alternatives can be complete without the other. The senses are in effect superior tools, but beauty in its many forms exists only in the mind. That realisation was my final diploma in art education, thanks to my friend Charles.

We continued to meet, as before. When I introduced my future wife, Charles took her hand in one of his, and with the other traced, naturally and without embarrassment to either of them, the lines of her face and the contours of her body. "You are beautiful, my dear", he said; " and you will make my friend Young a good wife. Don't forget to visit me as often as you can." The girl stooped and gently kissed him. "Thankyou, Charles, " she whispered; " I hope I may always be your friend, too".

And so it was, but always was not for long Within the year, after my wife and I had settled in our own cottage in the village, I found Charles one day in his usual comfortable chair, asleep for ever. His eyes were open and directed towards the wall on which hung the three paintings which had been such an important part of my art education. The smile on his lips was that of a wanderer who has come home at last after a long and dangerous journey. I closed his poor, blind eyes and with tears in my own went to phone the doctor and break the news to my wife. She was pregnant now, and I knew that she would bear me a son, and that his name would be Charles.

SEVENTEENTH SUMMER

A long train pulled breathily into a mainline station way into the West Country, and came to a halt amid snorts, squeals, smoke and steam. At two o'clock in the morning there were few people about except a comatose night shift of station staff. Only one person dismounted onto the platform, where he immediately rushed off to the guard's van to receive a dark-red touring bicycle, just in time to prevent it from catching in the crack between platform and running board. As he wheeled the bike towards the exit, a green flag waved perfunctorily and the train huffed its way into the night.

After consulting a map, the cyclist mounted and pedalled off down the street, following occasional signs pointing to "The Coast". He was neither a young man nor a boy, but in that 'between' stage which follows the initial period of transition named from the numbers between twelve and twenty, though in fact usually over long before the end of the second decade. Gerald was just seventeen and had left school with the promise of a minor scholarship to university. At that point in time he had not recovered from the double relief of passing his exams and leaving school, where he had not always been happy. Should he take up the scholarship, which meant waiting a year, and defer his National Service until after university, or should he get the army over first? In either case, he needed to find work for a year.
But this was a family holiday, perhaps even his last ever. His parents, two sisters and Aunt Annie (really a great-aunt) had already travelled down by car on the previous afternoon. There had been no room in the car for him, and doing it this way meant a certain amount of freedom as to when, where and with whom he ordered his comings and goings during his stay on the coast. He would be the only one with a bike, to start with. Not that he disdained the company of his great-aunt, though she of course was no longer a cyclist. Perhaps she had been in her youth, because her relationship with her great-nephews and nieces was one of mutual liking and respect based on her understanding of the attitudes, phases and general problems of the young. But then she had been a schoolteacher, and a very good one at that, and had devoted her life to her calling, never having married.

The night was fine, cool but not cold, and drying up after a series of showers. Having established which direction he should take to pick up the main road route to the sea, Gerald set off at a steady, rhythmic pace, timing his power-thrusts on the pedals to form a sort of syncopation with the uneven hum of the lamp-dynamo on his rear wheel. There was another advantage to this travelling separately - his luggage had gone in the car. The portly crescent of the moon was intermittently visible through the scattered clouds, but its light alone did not help much in showing him the way. He reckoned that he had about 35 miles to go - no problem, as on one occasion he had managed 140 miles in one day. He pedalled steadily on, not rushing but not hanging about, pausing sometimes when dazzled by infrequent oncoming lights, or when passing through an occasional village. It would be dawn in about another couple of hours, he estimated, and it would be another couple before he could reasonably expect there to be any sign of life in the guest house in which the family was staying.

It was for that reason that a sudden snapping sound and a clinking of metal on metal did not send him into a panic when he discovered that the bracket on which his front lamp was mounted had broken off and the lamp was hanging by its power-supply wire. It took only a moment to establish that without either tools, strong tape or a spare part a repair of any sort was not possible. Shrugging his shoulders, Gerald remounted and rode, more slowly than before, holding the lamp in one hand with a couple of fingers still on the handlebar. At least there was no deadline to meet; it was just awkward, began eventually to be a bit painful, and was in general a damned nuisance.

Once dawn broke, he picked up speed slightly and arrived at his destination with an hour or so to kill. This he occupied by spying out the land. The promenade, with its long stretch of golden sand below; a small pier which looked no better and no worse than average; some tennis courts which might be useful if he could find someone to play with. In fact, his mother was pretty good if it came to that. A few early risers were beginning to filter down to the front when he turned inland and rode slowly towards the street in which he would make his home for the next few weeks. His mother and sisters were already up and waiting for him, glad he had arrived and sympathetic about the lamp-bracket, which he was able to get replaced later that day.

The two girls took no time at all to fit comfortably into the new routine of playing on the beach, taking frequent dips in the sea, and trips out in the car every other day or so. Gerald joined in some of this fun, but preferred sometimes to wander off on his own. At school he had not graduated to the eminence of having a regular girl-friend from one of the local girls' high schools. In fact, despite having two sisters, he was not shaping up at all as a ladies' man. He thought about girls, but from rather an unsteady and inadequate base. The superficial facts of life he knew. He was familiar with the tremendous range of female form and features, and perhaps because of that had unconsciously developed an idea of his ideal girl which was not often matched up to, possibly because it was personal, fastidious and extremely specific. His main crush at school (a boys-only establishment) had been on a tall, beautiful girl a couple of years his senior, who dressed like a relict of the 1920s in leopard-skin coat and gloves and moved like the graceful feline predator which she may possibly have proved to be, had Gerald ever got near her.

After a week of the holiday there had been no sign of a young lady who came anywhere near the exacting specification, but fortunately among the new arrivals was a young man, fully-fledged and therefore several steps ahead of Gerald. Jonathan had come down with his mother. He was very tall, unlike Gerald; his hair was blonde rather than just on the fair side, like Gerald's, and he was, to Gerald's jealous eye, extremely handsome. Setting aside the fact that at this point in his life Gerald had absolutely no inkling of the concept of male love, it might have been thought that he was attracted by a distinct resemblance in style between Jonathan and Binkie, the young lady in the leopard-skin coat.

However, it turned out that Jonathan was an excellent tennis-player- almost up to county standard, in fact. It was a huge boost to Gerald's ego that on the court the two, despite their totally different playing styles, were pretty evenly matched. And on the rare occasion when two other players of similar standard were available, Jonathan and Gerald made a very difficult team to beat. Thus, a pleasant friendship developed between the two, destined to outlast the holiday by many years.

Jonathan's mother both fascinated and repelled Gerald. She had been an actress, and her constant claim to fame was to have appeared with Ronald Colman. Having had absolutely no experience of stage folk, Gerald did not know quite what to make of this larger-than-life lady, who called him darling before they had become properly acquainted and looked at close quarters old enough to be his grandmother. It didn't matter, however. Jonathan was good company and himself sufficiently different to be a permanent source of interest and wonder to Gerald.

Because of the limited space in the car, the two lads never got to go together on one of the day-trips, but to Gerald these were always worth going on, covering as they did a good few miles in different directions and taking in many coastal and inland villages and beauty spots. On one particular day the destination was a small fishing village known the world over for its quaint beauty and the artistic community which in consequence it supported. When the family arrived there, the girls made a beeline for the beach, while Gerald wandered round the village admiring the ancient cottages, the old boats drawn up on the tiny apron of sand in the small, near-spherical bay, and the general atmosphere of timeless tranquillity which even the hordes of tourists could not entirely dispel. It was perhaps this sense of peace which aroused in him the realisation that he was somehow not at peace with himself. His boy's mind, subconsciously reaching for adulthood, had become restless and dissatisfied. He desperately needed a token that he was an individual ready to take his place in the world.

Gerald made his way across the narrow low headland at one side of the harbour and found there a point at which smooth rocks gave access to the sea. He changed into his bathing trunks, left his clothes in a pile on the rocks, slid into the water and struck out for the open sea. He was a competent though not experienced swimmer, and the tide was coming in on small wavelets which sparkled as flecks of foam caught the sunlight. He swam parallel to the headland until he was far enough out to move across the seaward end of the cliffs and turn into the bay itself. In front of him he could just make out, from the colours of their costumes, the tiny figures of his sisters still running noisily round the little beach. As he made his way steadily into the cove he found himself meeting a scattered sprinkling of fishheads, guts and tails thrown overboard by the incoming fishermen and left to wash around until they were either carried out to sea or scavenged by the various creatures which inhabited the bowl of water between the twin headlands. Gerald was a touch on the fastidious side, and was not happy about all this debris, especially when he thought about the potential danger from piscivorous denizens of the deep which might be attracted into the cove. Still, the water was not that deep, so he ploughed on and soon felt his feet touch ground. He waded the rest of the way to the beach, causing hardly any interest among the few people there. The fishermen lounging on the quay regarded him with slight curiosity, but his sisters scarely noticed his approach until he grabbed them suddenly from behind and shouted "Bo!" His parents did not hear of the exploit until he told them years later. The next day, though Gerald never heard about it, a monster conger eel was caught off the headland round which he had swum. By the time he had recovered his clothes and changed back into them, the family was gathered up and loaded back into the car. Auntie Annie, who had been to the village several times before, had enjoyed a lovely day sitting in a deckchair at the top of the beach or plodding slowly round the alleyways, where she had with great daring purchased and consumed in the street an ice cream.

The rest of the holiday went by with little change of pace, except that Jonathan and his mother went home and Gerald's father returned to the office, so that a car trip became a thing of the past. The only real highlight was a visit to a typical seaside show by a typical seaside concert party. Gerald was not particularly impressed in general but was rather tickled by the comedian, who asked the audience what steps they would have taken if, during the war they had seen a German parachutist descending towards them "Bloody big ones", shouted a Cockney voice, amid roars of approving laughter. But even that little bit of nonsense failed to lift the cloud of introspective doubt, self-pity and loneliness which had hovered above Gerald's head since the swim round the headland. He no longer had the company of Jonathan, and his mind turned again to girls and the unfathomable delights which, according to a thousand books, they conferred upon any male lucky enough to attract their attention. His thoughts were one huge farrago of romantic love, physical beauty, boon companionship and veiled sexuality. And there was no girl there to walk with him, perhaps even holding his hand; to talk with him, complementing his brilliant conversation with compliments and admiration; and in effect just being there to give him the feeling of being a complete man rather than an insecure, desperate boy. On his last evening he stood in the dusk, leaning against the promenade railings and gazing first out to sea and then along the front as if hoping that the ideal girl would suddenly turn the corner and, waving and smiling, come towards him and take his arm. His by now massive inferiority complex did not permit him to hope for more. As he stood there, a fragment of verse ran through his head, tripping and skipping in just that rhythm with which his girl might have come to him:-

The lights on the water are gleaming; soft, dark air hangs warm on my head; the night's too young for parting, but my heart is dead.
Happiness dances around me - blithe laughter and words left unsaid; the night's too sweet for parting, but my heart is dead.
The whole world is weary within me as I drag my way home to my bed; the young night and I are parting, for my heart is dead.

Gerald took one last look at the dark sea and the velvet sky, and turned for home. Somehow he felt better. Maybe the sudden realisation that perhaps, after all, he could feel adult feelings and think adult thoughts had also made him accept that at last he was standing on the threshold between boyhood and manhood and that, uncertain and unknown though the future might be, there was no turning back. Gerald whistled as he walked briskly home to his lodgings, and began to plan his first steps in the new life which had opened up like a delicious panorama before him.

THE BATTLE OF WATERLOO ROAD

There stood some years ago in a small Northern town two grocery stores, more or less opposite on either side of a busy thoroughfare whose origin lay in a commemoration of the great battle in which the final hopes of Napoleon Buonaparte were destroyed. The establishments were operated by two widowers, Mr Hobson on the west side and Mr Pitts on the east. The road between them had almost the significance of an international frontier along which the constant traffic of trams, carts and motor-cars acted the part of a vigilant customs patrol in rendering the crossing of the road a very difficult and dangerous operation. Mr Hobson had one child, a son Edward (often called Teddy), and attended the ancient Parish Church situated not far behind his shop. Mr Pitts, on the other hand, patronised the Bethesda Chapel a few yards along the road, and had one daughter, Nancy. For the record, the wives had been half-sisters.

Because the shops were no more than a few yards apart, competition was to be expected, but in fact was neither as necessary nor as fierce as might have been thought. The road between them acted very much as a barrier between east and west, and in each direction there was a substantial hinterland of small, residential streets with little, terraced houses packed with children whose playgrounds were in the back alleyways which divided the rows of dwellings. Thus, the folk who lived to the east tended to patronise exclusively the shop of Mr.Pitts, while those to the west used mainly the establishment of Mr.Hobson, neither group having to venture across the concrete strip laced with steel tram-lines which divided them. There was another apportionment, too, in that whenever possible churchgoers shopped with Hobson, and chapel people with Pitts.

Nonetheless, the finer points of competition were not neglected by either side. Let Mr.Hobson display a colourful iron sheet proclaiming the merits of Lyons' tea, and within a few days there would appear resplendent outside the shop of Mr.Pitts a similar contraption advertising the virtues of Lipton's. Direct advertising was one thing, but the battle lines being so firmly drawn, it was obvious that special measures were going to be needed if either side was to gain just a single small advantage. It was Mr. Hobson who first turned his attention to the question of display, alerted to its possibilities by a chance remark from one of his customers, who commended him on the enticing look of a pile of tins of peas and corned beef, tastefully arranged to form the semblance of a flower. On the following day Mr. Pitts was startled to note, dimly through the open door opposite, a military line of menacing cheeses frowning from behind the counter, while small packets of condiments and spices strategically placed below them gave the impression of a myriad mice scurrying anxiously around the lumbering feet of a ponderous herd of elephants. He was not slow to react, and before long his cheese section, cunningly cut into wedges and squares, was seen to resemble nothing less than a thick, yellow theorem of Pythagoras.

Acting on the premise that attack can be a profitable form of defence, Mr.Pitts devised a new strategy which involved extending the hours during which his shop was open for business, and Mr. Hobson, having one evening locked his front door and started to clean up, was dumbfounded to see customers still drifting in and out of the premises opposite. He could not do otherwise but flatter his rival by imitating his latest ploy, and once more the two were on level pegging.
Competition by price was never contemplated by either adversary. For a start, in those days and in that town it was just not done; secondly it could prove disastrous to the cash flow of a business, and neither of the two grocers was prepared to risk finding customers buying in both shops and taking advantage of the discounted prices from time to time on offer in each place. Besides, it was obvious that while the overall situation would remain in exactly the same balance the size of each day's turnover in both establishments would diminish. A situation of stalemate was admitted on both sides.

There was no acrimony in the conflict. Both Hobson and Pitts had a good business and neither wished to compromise it for the sake of one-upmanship. On several evenings serious discussions took place between father and son and father and daughter. Both Nancy Pitts and Teddy Hobson were junior partners in their respective family enterprises, and both knew that before too long the businesses would be theirs. Teddy was a mere six months older than Nancy, and quite apart from their relationship through their respective half-sister mothers the two had gone to school and grown up together, receiving an equally excellent education into the grocery business from their fathers. There, however, their narrowest loyalties ended.

Nancy attended the chapel perfunctorily, and Teddy went to church because his father wanted him to do so for business reasons. But in their rare moments of leisure they had had reached an understanding one with the other, completely unknown to their fathers. The relationship was not yet at the stage where the risk of upsetting their parents might be justified. Teddy knew that Nancy hankered after her own business in hairdressing and the growing field of beauty treatment and preparations, while Nancy was sure that Teddy had progressive leanings and yearned to introduce new, different and daring selling methods into his father's shop.   The fact that the pair had been in effect "walking out" together for several years went a long way to prove that the war between their fathers was little more than a private game played for the sheer delight of winning points from each other.   Although the two men took great care not to be seen to be friendly, in fact they remained in private on the same easy, christian-name terms as when their spouses were still alive.   Underneath it all, each nursed the ambition to leave to his offspring a better business than the other could do.   It was a war of attainment rather than attrition.

The status quo dragged on for some considerable while, until a totally unconsidered factor entered into the equation.   Four hundred yards up the road there opened a new, large, modern and progressive store, one of the many similar businesses which sprang from the Co-operative movement.   Teddy and Nancy were sent by their respective parents to spy out the land, and it was not unnatural that they should make the first move in each other's company.   It took but five minutes to realise that this was competition with a capital C.   Two separate councils of war were held that night, directed for the first time not against the rival opposite but against this new, terrible, powerful joint opponent.
The children counselled an alliance of necessity, but the parents were too entrenched in their own long-term positions to wish to adopt such a radical solution.   Both, in different ways, made the same comment.   "I'm getting on, you know, Nancy, " said Mr. Pitts, " and things have never been the same since your mother died. The heart sort of went out of me and it's been only the thought of your future that's kept me going."   Across the road, Mr Hobson was saying to Teddy :- " I just can't bring myself to do it, lad.   You can't teach an old dog new tricks, you know.   Besides, I've not been feeling all that spry lately and an upheaval like that might lay me out altogether."
A further, smaller discussion took place the following day, between the two representatives of the younger generation, whose future to a degree was at stake.   "Nance", said Teddy, "I'm worried sick. If we don't get together, we're sunk. And if we do Dad won't have his heart in it. Whatever happens, I want him to enjoy some sort of retirement, not die shovelling sugar or slicing bacon. He's been good to me since Mum went."   Nancy nodded.   "I know how you feel, love," she said.   "Mine's just the same. If only we could bring them together properly again. They used to get on pretty well in the old days, especially when they went fishing or played cards."   Teddy was silent , his forehead wrinkled with concentration.   "Have you got any money saved? " he asked.   "Quite a bit, "

replied the girl; "I've never really had much time to spend it." "Me too", agreed Teddy; "That gives me an idea. Supposing we bought a small house where they could live together and we took over the shops - still keeping them as financial partners, of course?" Nancy considered this. "Sounds fine", she answered. "Right ", continued Teddy. "Of course you'll have to marry me. Two can live cheaper than one." "What gives you the idea I want to ", she flared, tossing her pretty head. "I know you, " her suitor riposted, "You'd do anything if it was good business". She grinned. "You could be right, at that," she said. "O.K., you're on. But we need to get everything else settled first."

Six months later, the Co-Op store was flourishing, but the Pitts's grocery shop was shut. Closed, that is, as a food store. Instead, the premises had an entirely new look. Upstairs, the living quarters where Nancy had been born, her mother had died and her father had bravely carried on to do his duty by his daughter, had been refurbished and now housed the specialist hairdresser who managed that side of the business below. Through the new plate-glass windows of the shop downstairs could be seen an array of basins and mirrors before which sat a row of local ladies anxious to improve the appearance of their hair according to the latest fashion and thus steal a march on their friends and neighbours. On the other side of the room, Nancy Hobson, as she now was , presided over shelves and cabinets full of mysterious jars and bottles with enticing labels, full of this, that or the other preparation guaranteed to prevent or remove wrinkles, soften skin weathered by fifty years of exposure to the elements and to the smoke and grime of industry, or to superimpose on an average, homely female face the image of one of the sirens of the cinema screen. Because it was the only one of its kind in the area, the establishment attracted a multi-denominational clientele which came from all points of the compass, even braving the crossing of Waterloo Road. The desire for self-improvement, and for something new and different was, it seemed, a passport which took its owner through the frontier of previously unexplored territory.

Across the road, Hobson's Provisions Emporium also had a new look and a new sense of bustle and urgency. Teddy had introduced many of the new methods after which he had been hankering for some years. The marble food counters were now protected by glass surrounds. Anti-fly screens predominated in areas which displayed naked foodstuffs. Teddy and his assistants wore gloves for the handling of such produce. Around the other walls of the store were shelves on which a carefully selected range of tinned and packeted goods was displayed for self-service before payment at a new till actually manned (or rather womanned) by a smart and pretty cashier. These shelves were clearly and logically marked as to the type of goods on any particular section. Prices, too were unequivocally displayed, and these in themselves were an attraction, monitored and adjusted as they were in relation to those charged elsewhere in the town. A judicious mix of "Quality First" and "Never Knowingly Undersold" was attained. Regular special offers at discounted prices were a feature; credit accounts and deliveries were available for selected customers; and a Christmas Club could be joined by anyone prepared to contribute regularly from March to December in return for a bonus of a medium-sized Christmas pudding.

Above all, the old standards of personal service were not only maintained but improved upon. Superintending, as well as serving, stood Teddy Hobson attired in a straw boater and a spotless white overall coat lovingly prepared for him by his wife and clean each day. He would greet each regular customer by name, ask after her family and converse soberly while purchases were being chosen and wrapped in clean paper, greaseproof of course for fresh food. From casual shoppers he would personally ascertain their wants and offer assistance and explanation of how these might best be satisfied. An atmosphere of efficiency, friendliness and courtesy pervaded the whole shop. And accordingly it prospered.

Nancy and Teddy excused themselves by pressure of business from regular attendance at their respective places of worship, but took care to show their faces occasionally and contribute generously towards special appeals for funds.

The two elderly gentlemen were perfectly contented in their compact but comfortable house, from which they sallied forth regularly on early morning fishing expeditions. The most important item of furniture in their living-room was a card table on which stood a magnificent cribbage board and sets of chessmen, draughts and dominoes, a retirement present from their children. They lacked only one thing - the knowledge that their interlinked family line would carry on after they were gone, but they did not fail to take comfort from the occasional gleam in Nancy's eye when she contemplated her husband's aura of business success. This, they agreed between themselves, promised equal achievement shortly in other, more leisurely and personal activities.

So ended the gentle, bloodless battle of Waterloo Road. After it there remained lessons taken from the book of proverbs - not the Biblical one. " A penny saved is a penny gained; all is not lost that is in peril; business is business; if you desire peace, prepare for war; love will find a way; necessity is the mother of invention; nothing venture, nothing win; there are two sides to every question; times change and we change with them; cut your coat according to your cloth; two heads are better than one; what's sauce for the goose is sauce for the gander;

when one door shuts, another opens; where there's a will there's a way; youth will be served; and you never know what you can do until you try."

Certain other sayings were disproved, for instance:- "two of a trade never agree" and "youth and age will never agree." But perhaps, in the circumstances, the most apt proverb of all was "Keep your shop and your shop will keep you."

SANCTUARY

Jack Evans walked stealthily up the hill towards the neat little stone cottage near the crest The red of the dawn sky was fading as the day took shape, bidding to be clear and perhaps sunny. Evans was on the run, and he was a dangerous man. A killer to whom the termination of a human life was of no more significance than stepping on an ant, he did not yet know that he had recently killed again. An evening diversion engineered from outside by gangland elements endeavouring to spring one of their leaders had given him a split-second chance to free himself, and he had taken it. In the process a warder who got in his way had been ruthlessly chopped down and had since died in hospital. The break had taken place some thirty-six hours previously, but Evans still did not feel safe, though he had so far managed to cover his tracks quite efficiently. Now he needed food, clothes and money, and this small home on the edge of the moors was isolated enough to make it a possible source of those commodities.

A wisp of smoke curled upward from the chimney pot and drifted quietly away to merge with the purple haze of the heather which was the main inhabitant of the bleak hills stretching into the distance towards the backbone of the country. Someone was obviously up and about, a conclusion confirmed immediately as an elderly man emerged from the back door to deposit a panfull of ash in a nearby dustbin. When the man had gone back inside, Evans crept up to the cottage and found that the door had not been re-locked. He burst into the kitchen, where the man and his frail wife were sitting down to breakfast. He did not even bother to speak, but struck the old man a vicious blow which knocked him to the floor, on which his head banged with a thump like a bass drumbeat. The old lady gazed with horror on the spectacle of her husband's blood seeping out onto the tiles, and bent down to help him. The effort proved too much for her and she subsided gently into an unconsious heap on the floor.
Evans swiftly ransacked the cottage, concentrating entirely on his needs. Food he found in plenty in the larder, and took bread, cheese, a meat pie and a can of lemonade, which he stuffed into a haversack hanging behind the interior door. A tweed jacket from the bedroom fitted him fairly well, so he took also a couple of shirts, a pair of trousers and some stout boots. There was not much money about, but what there was in the old man's wallet and his wife's handbag Evans extracted and thrust into his pockets. Then without delay he ran from the building, first checking to make sure that no-one else was in sight.

Moving carefully and trying either not to make tracks or to erase those that he did make, he disappeared up the hill. Finding in a ditch a stream with a little water trickling down he sloshed along for a hundred yards or so, before climbing out by a clump of bushes, where he changed into the purloined clothes, thrusting his own back into the haversack for disposal later on. He continued cautiously onward towards the brow of the hill.

Within a minute of Evans' emergence from the cottage, by which time he was in the ditch and outside sounds were muffled, a small car drove up to the cottage. The driver was a man in his forties, dressed in overalls which did not hide his muscular physique and a cap below which his clear eyes in a clean-shaven face gave a hint of intelligence and honesty. The rather pretty woman with him, of similar age, was his wife and the daughter of the elderly couple in the cottage. The husband was on his way to work at an isolated site beyond the hill, while the wife had come to spend the day with her parents. She called out, knocked at the door and immediately entered. Her startled shout brought her husband quickly into the kitchen. Having been a soldier and seen active service, he knew something about wounds, as indeed did his wife, who had trained as a nurse. He could see that his mother-in-law had merely fainted but was probably suffering from severe shock, while the old man had split his head open and would require expert medical attention, and might even so die from his wound. His army training came to the fore. "Liz", he commanded, "Phone the ambulance and the police and get them up here as quickly as possible. I saw something move on the other side of the brook and I'm going to have a look round". The woman did not demur, but replied simply "Be careful, Tom".

The man ran through the small garden and started to mount the hill. He knew the ground well, for his works were no more than half-a-mile away. He was, in fact, a crane-driver at a large scrap-metal processing and recovery plant which spread untidily over the hillside beyond the crest and was at least invisible from a distance, though an unquestionable eyesore in such beautiful but bleak surroundings. There was no proper perimeter fence, but a secure inner compound contained an office and some of the machinery essential to such an operation. That week it was Tom's job to open up, so there was nobody else about. Further down the slope, a movement caught his eye, and he could see a crouching figure among a debris of crumpled cars. As he watched, a man climbed into a vehicle which still retained its rear shape.

Jack Evans was tired. He had not slept for two nights and he needed to rest quietly and plan his next move. Not uneducated, he remembered how in his childhood he had loved so much the thrilling, electric feeling of sanctuary when during a storm he could nestle alone, still warm and dry, in a hollow tree or close to the heat of a fire within the flimsy windowpane which separated him from the garden where the elements howled impotently for his blood. He had changed a lot since then, he reflected. He settled down with a sigh on to the rear seat cushions of the car and fell quickly into a deep sleep on which the sounds of the outside world made little impression.

Tom moved rapidly to the compound and unlocked the gate. It had not escaped his notice that the car which now held Jack Evans was within reach of a large magnet-crane . He knew at once, from newspaper accounts, who the other man must be. And he knew also that Evans was a cold-blooded killer who according to the Old Testament rules of decent human conduct should not have been allowed to live as a serious danger to the community as a whole. As a soldier, death was no big deal for him personally. He had killed, too, but within the rules. The law, with which he did not entirely agree, had spared this treacherous animal who had callously attacked his wife's father and had quite possibly added his death to the catalogue of crime which had been listed in the papers. He had no doubt that if Evans knew that he had been discovered he would not hesitate to kill again. He - Tom- was not prepared to allow himself to be butchered simply to avoid breaking the ridiculous law which could allow a victim defending himself, his family or his property to be sued for assault. If his father-in-law died in such dreadful circumstances, Liz would be desolated and her mother would not survive for long, either. Yet another death, and untold unhappiness, to be laid at the door of the sleeping killer below.

Trained as he was to make instant decisions on the basis of whatever information was available on the spot, Tom acted according to his instincts and his feelings for his family. As quietly as he could he ran to the huge crane and started its engine. The massive magnet-head swung to a position above the car and descended in silence until Tom's expert control lowered it with scarcely a sound on to the car roof. He activated the magnet, carefully raised the car and, swinging the load round, deposited it in the hopper of the powerful compactor which could reduce a large car to the size of a crate. The compactor could be worked by remote control from the crane and with a firm qualm-free finger Tom depressed the switch. The sound of tortured, buckling metal lasted no longer than a few seconds, and no other sound intruded. Engaging the magnet once more, Tom lifted the chunk of metal which was now also a coffin and moved it to a pile of similar chunks which would eventually be carted away and buried deep at sea. Then he switched off all the machinery which he had used.

In ten minutes or so Tom's workmates began to arrive. He excused himself quickly on the grounds of his father-in-law's accident and returned to the cottage. Liz was more than pleased to see him, for she had done a bit of mental arithmetic herself and linked the situation to the escaped convict who was currently occupying so much press space. "Did you see anything", she asked anxiously. "No", replied Tom. "Must have been a bird or something. But I went right down to the works and opened up, just in case. What about the ambulance and the police?" "Both on their way," said Liz, "But Dad doesn't look too good". "Don't worry , love," said Tom. "He'll be O.K.as soon as he gets to hospital". He wished that he felt as confident as he sounded, but at least the old man was fit and well and hospitals could work wonders sometimes. "You go with your Mum and Dad", he added. "I shall have to stay and talk to the police. I'm pretty sure it must have been that escaped convict we've been reading about, and they will want to know. He must have got clean away before we got here."

As Liz and her parents were driven rapidly away to the hospital, and Tom was doing his duty as a citizen and helping the police with their enquiries, a tiny drop of red appeared at the corner of one of the unsightly metal blocks waiting patiently for their transport to the oblivion of the ocean. Nobody saw and nobody connected it with the disappearance of a wanted criminal.

The unquestioning sea would receive his coffin and the land would be better off without him, in the secret knowledge that human justice could still intervene when villainy seemed to be riding roughshod over common decency.

THE POWER OF THE DOG

Why do you come when I call, your ears cocked to hear what I'm saying?
Why do you bring me your ball, ever hopeful and ready for playing?
Why wriggle under a chair after digging a hole in the garden,
then tear round and leap in the air at the first indication of pardon?
Why do you worry my leg, growling to tell me I'm bitten,
then suddenly break off and beg or roll on the floor like a kitten?
Why do you bother to show the pleasure it gives you to heed me?
Animal, surely you know I need you as much as you need me.

Tip reluctantly removed his nose from its quest into an old tin can under the hedge. He looked round and, seeing his master several yards in front of him down the road , scampered to catch up. Tip was a dog of many colours, a regular dreamcoat of a dog His ancestry was as much of a mystery as that of many of the unfortunate children who in years gone by had received the blessing of good fortune at the Foundling Hospital in Coram fields. Collie there was, Jack Russell there was, fox terrier, whippet and spaniel there may well have been, and the net result was a tireless energy, a surprising burst of speed over a short distance, a superabundance of intelligence, an undying devotion to his people and a fierce independence far too highly-developed for his own good. If it suited him, Tip could walk to heel as though his nose was attached to his man's boots. If it suited him he would sit, come or stay with the best of them. Fortunately for his doggy dignity he had never been expected to balance sugar lumps on his nose or to die for his country, but without doubt he could effortlessly have acquired those skills.

Poor Tip! Notwithstanding all his many talents it was his destiny to be that most annoying and aggravating variety of canine characters - a Mitcher. Deep in his brain there lurked a primeval call of the wild, which struck swiftly and without warning and sent him haring off into the nearest woodland where, sometimes for several days at a time, he would apparently join forces with foxes or in other ways revert to his wild roots. Then, as swiftly as it had come, the madness would leave him and he would return home, unkempt, bedraggled and on his knees, but still able to wag his tail with pleasure, even at the threat of a walloping from his relieved owner. At times the call would come at night and Tip would decamp from his warm, protected straw bed in the garden shed and, with a few chilling howls at the moon, if there happened to be one, he would leap up into the apple-tree, tightrope-walk along the branch which projected over the next-door land, jump lightly onto the garage roof and so down to freedom in the wild woods. It did little good for access to the apple-tree to be restricted with wood or metal bars.. Tip would simply bite through the chicken-wire along the base of the fence and get out that way. If it pricked or cut his nose, so what. It was no worse than having a snout full of hedgehog prickles, which he frequently did, never having learned not to try and play ball with the curled-up little animals; obviously the legacy of his ancestry over-ruled his native intelligence when it came to things like hunting, tracking and sheer untrammelled animal enjoyment.

Of certain pleasures Tip never tired, no matter how often he sampled them. He had a universal reputation in the locality as a ladies' man (I suppose that might translate into 'bitch's dog'), and sometimes his master would have to fend off indignant approaches from other dog-owners. "You should keep that damned dog of yours under control. My Lassie (or Diana, or Phoebe, always a pedigree animal several sizes too large for Tip) is a fine, obedient dog, but that wretched fleabag of yours entices her out." As if it was Tip's fault. He couldn't help being rakish, devil-may-care, over-sexed and good-looking; indeed at the one dog-show for which his owner was rash enough to enter him he had refused to do what he was told, snarled menacingly at the judge, but still come away with a rosette for the most handsome dog in the show.

There was proof positive of his intelligence and his independent turn of thought. On more than one occasion he had been called to come in for his supper at about the time when one of his mad moments was imminent. He did not come, and he did not go, but pranced around just out of reach and his thoughts could be read in his eyes, in the angle of his head and in his stiff, coiled-spring movements. "I know that I should go in; there's a good meal waiting for me in my bowl. But trees and hidden paths and wonderful scents and the rustling of panicking small animals are there in the woods, and tonight the moon will be full and I will howl, and the foxes will join me, and I shall travel back in time to the days when every dog was his own master, subservient only to the pack-leader. And I can be leader of my own pack and the females will flock to me when I call and the whole world will be just a bone for dogs like me to gnaw, bury, dig up and gnaw again. No doubt there will be some sort of reckoning when I come home again, but WOOF! it will be worth it." And away Tip would run, his whole body alive with anticipated enjoyment and the graceful freedom of his forbears the wolves.

When Tip was in the prime and pride of his life, his world was dealt a severe blow. His mistress was no longer there to prepare his food, cuddle and caress him and talk sweetly to him as they walked together over the fields or sat cosily in front of the red warmth of a fire in the depths of winter. Some inner force prompted him to stay close to his distraught master and offer doggy sympathy which may well have been of more worth than all the letters and other expressions of condolence which flooded into the house. The two became even closer than they had been before, and the mitching gradually came to an end. There was still fun to be had in exercising the herding instinct which was strong in him, penning young cattle in the corner of a field and then wondering what the hell to do with them. Fun, too, when the trains on the small branch line close by would hoot to attract his attention as they approached the meadow in which he was running apparently aimlessly to and fro with his nose in the grass. The drivers knew Tip well, and delighted in slowing down before accelerating gently away until he was running at full stretch beside them, emitting breathless yips until the thick hedge at the end of the field stopped him and the train disappeared from view, tooting triumphantly.

On one of these morning walks, Tip's master was joined by a lady who was also enjoying the spectacle of the machine/canine contest. This first chance meeting became a regular event, not least because the lady had recently lost her husband after many happy years together. She, too relied heavily on animal companionship, in her case however a large cat named Tibby. Fortunately for all concerned, Tibby was not a walking cat. Not that Tip was unused to felines but his idea of play was rather too boisterous and damage to either or both might have resulted.

The lady lived at the far side of the village and, like Tip's master , nursed her grief quietly and alone, preferring not to join in the usual events and junketings of village life. Neither became involved in an amazing project which attempted to harness the entire resources, human and otherwise, of the village into a huge local Open Day, which included a Pageant of local history, a village fete, tea on the centuries-old lawns of some of the ancient cottages, now expensive show-pieces, and evening revelry to the sound of a jazzband in a marquee. Both, however, supported the event with their presence and small financial outlays on some of the sideshows. The lady, with a gleam, in her eye, encouraged Tip's master to participate in a dart-throwing stall, where a bullseye was rewarded by the removal of an article of clothing by a nubile young woman who was braving not only the prospect of near-nudity but the presence of the inclement weather which so often attacks such supposedly-summery occasions. Tip's master was not amused, but his protests were beaten down by the unanswerable example set by the local rector, who appeared to be expending the whole of the previous Sunday's collection at the stall, egged on by the cries of some of the lads of the village - "Good for you, Vicar!" "Gerremoff", and so on. The friendship between man and woman survived, but there was no hint of anything further.

Two years later, during which time communication between the two had been cordial but not particularly frequent, Tip's hourglass ran out. He had survived a brush with a motor-bike, various incidents involving other dogs, and the furious attentions of other dog-owners - his masculinity remained unimpaired despite his advancing age. Something had to give, however, and his sorrowing master found him one morning under a hedge in his garden, at peace and still handsome. Something of the will to carry on himself went out of the man as he buried his faithful companion in the garden from which Tip had so often escaped on his glorious journeys back to his roots. For some while, he became a recluse saved from self-pity only by the loyalty and understanding of his family who, though living too far away for frequent visits, kept in constant touch by telephone and made sure that their father was not left to brood on his loneliness.

One morning, while walking sadly in the fields and watching the now-silent train pass at uniform speed, the man became aware of footsteps hurrying to overtake him. It was his acquaintance and former dog-walking companion. "I've only just heard. I'm desperately sorry about Tip", she said. The man nodded. "I know how you feel," she continued. "I lost my Tibby six months ago and I'm still not really over it. Somehow it's worse than losing a human friend. Perhaps that's because animals are so dependent on you and get to be such a part of your life." The man nodded again. "It's hard", he said simply. "Why didn't you let me know sooner?", said his companion. "I don't really know," said the man. "I felt so lonely without him". "Will you get another dog", she asked. "No", he said. "It would never be the same. My wife loved him too." "Same with me," she replied. "So we're both in the same boat. What about forming a mutual consolation society; no strings, no recriminations, just company?" The man stopped, and looked at her for the first time since she had appeared at his shoulder. "Do you know," he said, "I think that's exactly the sort of thing my wife would have said. I'm game if you are, but you'll have to make allowances to start with." The woman took his hand. "My dear," she said, "I meant 'mutual'. We can but try, and if it doesn't work, there'll be no hard feelings from me. Do you fancy coming round for a meal tomorrow?" "I'll look forward to it," he said, and they walked hand in hand out of the field and into the sunshine of the village street, which seemed almost like a symbol of better days ahead.

FLYING DUTCHMAN

The Admiral stretched his still-lean frame and lazed back in his chair as he watched with pride his family around the table. His son, already a commodore in the Fleet; his tall, beautiful daughter-in-law, and his grandson who, having reached double figures had been promoted to the senior mess-table on special occasions. A scuffling and squeaking sound came from the floor below, where his small granddaughter was playing Star-Wars with her dolls. The young boy, still in awe of his grandfather, especially when the latter was in full dress uniform, spoke diffidently. "Tell me one of your stories, Grand-dad " he asked. The Admiral of the Space Fleet put down the tall, slim glass from which he had appreciatively been sipping, and watched briefly while the white, almost spiritual miasma formed again to hover above the rare and precious Arcturian liqueur. Then, after a further pause, he began to speak, slowly and reflectively.

It's more than forty years since I joined the service as a cadet, (he said), and in a year or two I shall be retiring. After that - well, before I die I'd like to see you, son, in my place as Admiral; and if you, youngster, decide to follow in our footsteps, what better than to watch your passing-out parade at the Academy, with you top of your Class. Time alone will tell. But, talking about time, in all my years in Space I've seen plenty of sights that scared the h... I mean living daylights out of me, but only once have I come across something which was so weird that curiosity got the better of fright.

I was a raw Lieutenant then, on my first voyage in that rank, and I needed all the help I could get. Fortunately for me, the Senior P.Os liked me and kept off my back the matelots who were noted for pushing new officers into nervous breakdowns. I got plenty of stick, but it was always diverted before it really got to me. So I learned quickly, and never came, like some, to give anything but respect and loyalty to the men under my command, just as I expected them to do for me.

Anyway, this trip we were on a routine patrol, still in the solar system, and the time was beginning to feel a bit heavy. Just after muster one morning an emergency shout came through on the tannoy - "Ware asteroids ten degrees to port". It was routine, or so everybody assumed - until I got to thinking about what I'd been told about asteroids at the Ack. Probably fragments of larger bodies, either thrown off during formation, or possibly on disintegration. Orbits as regular as clockwork, but with no set pattern relating to size or weight. Not particularly dangerous to inhabited planets, unless an inhabitant happens to be underneath one when it breaks out of orbit and falls. But can be dangerous to spacecraft, especially when orbiting in groups or clusters. Nothing worth salvaging - just chunks of rock or metal. Then it hit me. We were nowhere near any predicted asteroid belt or general activity. So why were they there?

I was watchkeeper, so I was already on the bridge. "Visual" I yelled, and there they were - just a few medium-sized bits looking just like any run-of-the mill asteroid. I was still curious. "Can you analyse at this distance?", I asked the Scanner. "Sure, boss" came back the answer. Within thirty seconds up it came on the screen:- Hardly any metal content. None of the usual rock types. The flying missiles seemed to be made of compacted vegetable material. "What the hell?" I thought. "This is too much for me". So I took the risk and called the skipper. He growled a bit when he got to the bridge. "Want your hand holding, sonny?", he said. I pointed to the screen analysis. "So,", he said; " what do you expect from asteroids.?" "Metal and igneous rock, sir", I told him. He looked again. "Hmmph. Chart their course backwards and find out where they've come from."

I gave the order and carried on thinking. Compressed vegetable matter. My eye caught the trash ejector button. That was it!! "Sir," I yelped, a couple of octaves up the scale. He cottoned on fast. "That's as good a guess as any", he said. "Get that backtrack speeded up. There must be another ship out there somewhere." The direction-finding was easy, and we altered course towards the estimated point of origin of these parcels of - er - garbage. The scanners were on full strength, but there was nothing to see, until we could make out a sort of hazy, misty area just hanging in space. "What in the name of all that's wonderful is THAT? " said the Skipper. It was for all the world like the miasma that forms over that Arcturian nectar in these glasses here. Faint, untouchable, eerie yet almost smelling of soul and spirit. We hove to, just short of the outer tentacles of the mist. There was still nothing formal to be seen. The skipper edged the foremost nose of the ship right up to the cloud-like area. Nothing happened, except that the mist receded, almost as if it didn't like being touched. "Circumnavigate!" snapped the boss. Slowly, in a clockwise direction, we edged around the outer rim of the cloud until the plot-chart told us we had gone 360 degrees to make a full circle. Nothing but mist had been visible the whole circuit. Again we stopped. "Any ideas, gentlemen?" said the captain.

Now, as a youngster I had always enjoyed reading legends and myths and stories of the unexplained, though by that time most things of that nature had been nailed down and slipped neatly into appropriate slots. But there was one that hadn't. "Ever heard of the Flying Dutchman, Captain?" I asked. He did a double-take. "I did once," he replied; "Remind me."

So I told him the old legend, going back hundreds of years to the days when the only ships sailed on water; how a sea-captain from the Netherlands had turned pirate, and terrorised the oceans of the world with a crew of villains as daring and as desperate as himself. He was ugly and vicious to start with, and he had a soul to match. With each example of ruthless piracy and total disregard for human life or dignity, his face grew darker and uglier, and in turn his soul shrivelled and stank until even his own men kept well away from him. He climbed, as if hand-over-hand up a rope, steadily up the scale of wickedness, face over soul, and soul over face. Not even his crew knew for sure what had driven him to this state, though there was some talk of a lovely woman who turned away from him because she could not live with his decision to take to piracy. For years he sailed on, until he and his crew were old in years beyond all the recognised boundaries. Then, the truth burst upon the tired and hapless sailors. Their captain had sold his soul in exchange for invincibility in battle and revenge in the knowledge that the woman who, as he considered, had deserted him would end her days in poverty and despair, with all her beauty vanished and no-one to comfort her and close her eyes in death. It was further said that the captain had outsmarted the devil and won a concession in the bargain. He and his crew would sail the sea for ever, or until he won the love of a good and faithful woman. Scores of luckless female captives had been granted a short stay of execution in the hope that one might end the torment of the Flying Dutchman; but none did, all preferring death to any sort of association with the monster who sought to enlist their aid.

"That's the legend, sir, for what it's worth." The captain stood a moment in deep thought, and turned to the duty helmsman, a man as old as the skipper and possibly with a year or two more by way of service. "Does that ring any bells with you, Bill?", he asked. The helmsman handed over to his deputy. "It does, skipper", he said; "On the old limited solar boats we used to hear about a captain right back in the early days of space, who vanished without trace - ship, crew and all. Van Hoyt, or something like that, his name was. The only thing that ever came out by way of news was that he'd seduced a commodore's daughter but wouldn't stand by her, and she'd cursed him to high heaven. He just laughed, but he never came back from his next voyage."

There was a shout from the scanner; "Captain! Quick! Look on the screen!" All heads turned, to see a shadowy shape looming through the cloud. "God help us", said the old helmsman; "That's a "B"Class ship, a hundred years old if it's a day!" For a couple of seconds the old ship hung there, behind the mist, and every man in front of the screen swore afterwards that it dipped its nose in salute. Then it and the drifting cloud were gone.

"And that vision", said the Admiral, "will go to the grave with every man jack who saw it. Believe in ghosts and spirits when we can fly out into the universe? A likely story! But here before you is a man who cannot but believe in something which he saw with his own eyes, in the company of dozens of hard-bitten spacers who would never turn a hair if confronted by a mob of Vegans howling for their blood." He slowly savoured the last drops from his tall glass. "There are more things in heaven and earth, Horatio -----; and I would defy Horatio Nelson himself to put a better explanation on what we saw that day. So, son, and you, young man, too:- never ever dismiss the evidence of your own eyes if it's confirmed in the presence of other sane men. Because something is beyond your current ken doesn't mean that it is necessarily impossible. If space can be warped, so can thought. Remember that, and you'll have the advantage of most other men and probably a good few alien species as well."

He turned to his grand-daughter, who seemed to be attempting to chop the arm off one of her dolls with a plastic knife. "WHAT on earth are you doing, young lady?" The little girl smiled sweetly up at him. "Grand-dad", she said, " I'm only trying to teleport Mary one bit at a time into the back room!"
In the circumstances, there was no answer whatsever to that.

BETTER LATE THAN NEVER

At thirty-five, Fred was a completely unremarkable and ordinary person - ordinary, that is, in the usual context of the word rather than in the Wild West sense of 'ornery'. He was Mr. Average, and not even merely that. He was Mr. C.R.U.P.H.I.B.S. Average - Mister Commonplace Run-of-the-Mill Unimpressive Pedestrian Humdrum Invisible Bog Standard Average. If they could have found a few more like Fred, the police would never have failed to get a result from identification parades; though conversely Fred as a villain would have been able to get away with most things short of literal murder. He worked in the packing department of a large mail order firm, and had done so since he left school. He was unmarried and lived in the small, ordinary terraced house which he had inherited from his parents, whose only child he had been. He kept his tiny garden neat without being the slightest bit interested in it, and his main hobby was naval history. This was an attraction of the unattainable. Fred had never served in the Navy and felt rather more than queasy on a riverboat going down the Thames. But he read greedily both fact and fiction on his pet subject - dry, academic histories, pages and pages of figures, silhouettes and pictures of all types of vessel from a clockwork paddle steamer to the latest in modern naval technology, and of course the many well-researched stories about Hornblower and his fictional contemporaries. He enjoyed average good health, he was neither mad keen on nor dismissive of the opposite sex, and his life generally was a simple happy average.

One street away, in a house very similar to Fred's, lived a young lady named Freda. She too had neither brother nor sister and had lost her parents early in life, inheriting the house from them. Freda was not exactly average but she was very much typecast. She was a little too plump, though rounded in the right places, and she had pleasant though somewhat moonish features framed by mousey hair to which she paid little attention. Her eyes, like the rest of her, were placid behind her large round spectacles. A keen ornitholgist - had one ever found occasion to look at Freda - would probably have been struck by something slightly owl-like about her. She was about the same age as Fred, and she too was unmarried. She worked as an audio-typist in the office of a small engineering firm, to which she travelled every day on the underground. Perhaps Freda was not quite as contented as Fred; her passion was also for books, but historical romances covering any period, and she varied this diet with an occasional foray into the field of torrid love-sagas designed for women, in which either faithfulness reaped its due reward or promiscuity enabled the authors to promote hints of lusts and desires of the flesh such as would have been more than enough for a woman of supreme sexuality and which, had they occurred in real life, would certainly have terrified ninety-nine percent of the readers concerned. There was always a ready supply of such novels to be found in charity shops; original sales in paperback were usually good, but the books rarely found a permanent home on a discerning bookshelf. Freda, however, was neither deceived nor particularly excited by this proto-pornography, though she welcomed it occasionally as an interlude in a dramatised account of an otherwise uninteresting period of history.

The two were slightly acquainted, often meeting on the same train on their separate ways home from work. Freda got on at the same stop as Fred, and if the train was full he would politely try and get a seat for her. If they met on the way back they would walk home together, usually chatting about their latest literary acquisitions. On one such walk homewards they were both surprised to find an overlap between their special fields. Coming on the following week at the local cinema was a historical romance, but not just any old tale. It was a story based on Lord Nelson and Lady Hamilton. Fred, with absolutely no motive other than courtesy and the desire to discuss Horatio as a naval hero, suggested that they might go together to see the film. Freda, similarly motivated but anxious to talk about female power behind great men, agreed instantly to this opportunity to expand on her theories about Emma. A date was arranged for the following week.

The trip to the cinema was a great success and both parties were very happy to repeat it. Books were exchanged, and soon visits were arranged to view each other's library. The workaday acquaintance blossomed into a genuine friendship such as can grow only from common interests and mature only in an atmosphere of liking and trust. Several months after the momentous first outing, the two were drinking coffee after supper at Freda's house, talking about the changes which had taken place over the past three hundred years in male-female relationships, and in particular about the marriages contracted by famous people. They disagreed amicably about the merits and demerits of early or late marriages - not that either of them was in any way qualified to speak with authority on the subject. "A woman matures quicker than a man," said Freda; "besides there's always the question of having a family." "Maybe so," replied Fred "but what about financial security and so forth; that comes better when a man is a bit older." "What you are saying, then," argued Freda, "is that there is no good in sharing a bit of hardship at the start for the sake of being free of a family before you get too old to enjoy that freedom?" "Not fair!", answered Fred." All I am saying is 'better late than never'." He paused, struck by a sudden flash of inspiration, and continued "Talking of which, Freda, how about you marrying me." There was a silence gravid with the sound of mental cogs meshing and whirling. Then Freda spoke:- " Yes, Fred, I should like that very much, please."

The wedding took place two months later, quietly in a registry office with only a few friends from each workplace present. The honeymoon was spent on the eastern edge of the New Forest, whence they could reach places like Winchester and Salisbury for Freda and Fred could see Portsmouth, with the 'Victory', the 'Warrior' and the 'Mary Rose'.

Six months later they were contentedly established in a new, slightly larger house a bit closer to the station, having sold both their own places and bought in joint names. They were very happy with each other's company in a planned existence which allowed for watching TV when any historical dramas or appropriate documentaries were on and for plenty of free time for reading. One bedroom had been turned into a library, with its walls completely lined with bookshelves. They were reading in bed one night when Freda put down her book and said "There's something I've been meaning to tell you since before we got married, Fred, and I think I should do it now." "Go,on, love," answered Fred, ""you know what I always say - better late than never". "That's just it!" she went on; " do you remember saying that to me when you asked me to marry you?" "Of course," protested Fred; " how could I forget a thing like that?" Freda giggled. " Fred, dear, the trouble was that I thought you'd said 'LAID'!"

TOUR DE FARCE

There must be many people who can point to one or more examples of hilarious absurdity in their lives. The most ridiculous yet enjoyable time that I can recall was when my wife Jill's Canadian cousins decided to pay a visit to the UK and look up some of their family roots. Whereas my own family is now fragmented and thin on the ground, my wife's relatives are still as numerous as the grains of sand on Blackpool beach, from which area many of them came.

This particular cousin, Nigel, was second generation Canadian, and almost a generation older than us. But he was very keen on his roots and his wife Betty shared his enthusiasm. He had been high up in the global executive of an American company specialising in the manufacture of plastic extrusions, and had retired with the wherewithal to gratify his whim to explore his family's past.

We first met the two of them, by arrangement and in the company of my brother-in-law and his wife, at a swish hotel not far from the American Embassy in Grosvenor Square. As might have been expected - though not necessarily ensured - an immediate rapport sprang up over a meal, and in a fit of enthusiasm I suggested (mainly out of courtesy) that Nigel and Betty might like to join us on a completely pot-luck UK tour on which my wife and I were planning to embark in a couple of days time. I was astonished and indeed disconcerted when, after a confirmatory look between them, they accepted with pleasure. So it was that on the Saturday we drew up outside the hotel, watched their luggage being loaded into our car, and drove off as a group of four comparative strangers on an unplanned trip into the complete unknown for our cousins and the jaws of chance for ourselves. Fortunately we had a largish car with a decent-sized boot - or, bearing in mind that two-thirds of its contents were now transatlantic, should I say "trunk".

Passing smoothly on to the Cromwell Road extension, we were soon on the M4 and quickly to the Windsor turn off; for Windsor was to be our first port of call. It was nearly our last. Betty got hold of the official guide book to the Castle and insisted on going through it word for word, room for room, picture by picture and chair by chair. Nigel and I exchanged understanding glances. We both knew that we had no accommodation booked for that night, and it was desirable that we should put a few extra miles between ourselves and London. At the rate at which our party (or rather Betty) was moving, we were likely to be in Windsor until next Wednesday - at least. Eventually Nigel managed to persuade his nuts-on-history spouse to give Windsor best and we took once more to the road, but not until well gone three o'clock.

My original objective was Bath, but I didn't want to bash straight down the motorway because both Nigel and Betty had already shown signs of falling in love with the green fields, hills and woods of the English countryside. I stopped at a telephone box and, armed with an AA guide I started to phone for rooms. First I tried the Cotswolds. Burford - nothing; Stow-on-the Wold - nothing; even Cheltenham - nothing. In desperation I tried Cirencester and found the last rooms in a hotel there - and these had to be one double and two singles. It was any port in a storm, so off we went having promised to arrive by 6.30 p.m. Then a minor disaster struck between the high banks of a country lane; we were giving our guests the countryside treatment par excellence. A flock of crows were gathered on the road dismembering an unfortunate ex-rabbit, and one of them, either gorged or half-asleep, or possibly both, failed to lift off in time to avoid the car. We struck the bird with one headlamp. It fluttered off cawing shrilly, and we heard the tinkle of headlamp glass falling into the roadway. Fortunately it was nowhere near lighting-up time so we carried on and reached Cirencester on the dot of 6.30. Sure enough, we were able to take a double room for Nigel and Betty, and two singles for Jill and myself. Mine was without en suite facilities, which served only to exacerbate its lack of matrimonial comforts. When Jill went to her room she found a minor problem; there was no bed. We discussed the possibility of both sleeping in the small single divan in my room, but the hotel staff rallied round apologetically and moved in the appropriate furniture. At least we had a good and part-liquid dinner.

The following morning we had to make an early start because before we left the headlamp glass had to be replaced. By chance there was a main dealer a couple of doors away and the necessary repair was made so that we are able to set off at 10 o'clock. Our destination was quite a way away. Our son and a friend were on an extended camping tour and were spending a few days near Builth Wells. We had arranged to meet them there in the afternoon. We crossed the Severn and the Usk and struck north for the Welsh mining valleys. The roads were scenic in their grim way, and slow because of the twists and turns and innumerable small communities which they served. We passed the silent slope of Aberfan, sorrowing for its lost generation of children, went through that town with the almost music-hall name - Merthyr Tydfil - and headed up through the Brecon Beacons. The scenery brought gasps of amazement from two people who had divided most of their lives between Toronto and Florida. At Brecon itself we took the more or less direct line of a B road which led straight into Builth Wells. It was three p.m. and we were an hour late, but fortunately the boys were waiting for us and after a quick snack in a sort of cafe in the town square which from its clientele must have reminded our cousins of a very down-market drug store cum soda fountain, we followed them to their camp site. It was raining steadily and their smallish tent was pitched in a field beside a stream which looked to me dangerously full. At least the tent was fairly dry and there was just room for six of us to squeeze inside. I have to say that I thought Nigel and Betty performed an act of supererogation in taking all this in their stride, especially considering their age. We drank tea from mugs, having laced it with whiskey from the flask which I had had the foresight to bring with me.

It was now 4.30, and we had a good hundred miles to go to Betws-y-Coed, where we had already booked a room for ourselves, on the recommendation of my parents, and subsequently upgraded to two rooms by telephone. We phoned again and told them we would be a bit late. The journey through Mid to North Wales would have been breath-taking had the weather been better. As it was, at least the rain avoided the necessity to stop frequently for scenic picture taking. Through Rhayader and Llanidloes we went, turning there onto a minor road which offered in fine weather a classic example of Welsh mountain scenery. A bit later, however, even through low cloud we could not miss the threatening black bulk of Cader Idris, the fabled Giant's Chair, with its Matterhornish peak hanging over the pass below.
Many, many years later Jill and I climbed the Cader, starting in brilliant sunshine but seeing little above 1600 feet. We ate our lunch, after trekking blindly through rain and low cloud, in the mountain hut at the summit, duly sad to read on a nearby memorial tablet of a local hill-running champion who had figured in several mountain rescues and then dropped dead himself during a race. At least, we thought, he was doing what he most wanted to do.

On through Dolgellau we drove, past Lake Bala and via another B road onto the A5, and thus into Betws-y-Coed. Without much difficulty we located the 'guest house' so fulsomely praised by my parents. Certainly the accommodation within the house was fine, and the breakfast next morning excellent. Fortune however was not favouring the brave (i.e. Jill and myself). It turned out that the couple occupying the room which we were to have taken needed through indisposition to stay on for an extra night. Could we help the proprietor to cope with this small problem? The coping consisted in sleeping in a tiny caravan in the back

yard. Faute de mieux, we agreed. It wasn't exactly comfortable, and we
certainly didn't sleep too well, but it was fun in its way - if you accept as fun the
impossibility of both lying on our backs at the same time. It was a case of either
vertical or horizontal stacking - take your choice. We took it, but I do not
propose to go into further detail.

Breakfast, as I have mentioned, was very good. Somewhat refreshed, we set off
again. First stop , of course , was the famous Swallow Falls, sated by the recent
rain (which had stopped by this time) and rushing and roaring merrily down
amid a cloud of spray. A pretty picture, but two cups of coffee could not ignore
the sound of running water and Jill and I were obliged within an unconscionably
short space of time after breakfast to head for the woods and relieve our
demanding bladders. Whether Nigel and Betty had had less coffee or possessed
stronger or larger internal arrangements, we did not stop to enquire.

We were heading first for Chester. This we reached in good time for lunch, and
our visitors were spellbound by the medieval aspect of the Rows, and especially
by the fortuitous presence of the Town Crier, the like of which they had never
seen before and certainly had not expected to see now. We lunched in a pub up
on the Rows. It was crowded, but we found a booth with four vacant seats
though already partly occupied. Jill, in her usual nosey north-country fashion
immediately entered into conversation with the other occupants and it transpired
that we had mutual acquaintances - a thing which happens to us more often than
might have been thought possible. I remember once going on holiday to a
holiday camp when our son was tiny and our daughter was only on the way, and
being met as we entered our chalet by stentorian cries from down the path. It was
a friend and his wife from a mile or so away from our home. In fact, we have
even met similar circumstances both in Portugal and in America. But I digress.
We enjoyed an excellent and reasonably-priced lunch. On the way back to the
car, Betty enquired from Jill "Did you know those people?" "Good Lord no!",
replied Jill. "Never seen them before". Betty was flabbergasted. "But", she said
" you English are supposed to be so stiff and reserved!" "Not the Lancashire
ones", replied Jill - a good move, because Nigel's roots, like hers, were in that
county.

This was a good time to point out that we were in fact now heading for
Lancashire - at least, the southern end of it. Again we had no need to phone
ahead, for Nigel's company had a factory near Wigan and maintained there an
executive flat. He had managed to obtain permission to use it for a couple of

nights. We arrived there by late afternoon, booked in past the security gate and were met by the manager of the plant. He showed us to our quarters. "Executive flat" wasn't in it. The works had been converted from a former Army barracks, and the "flat" had been the Commanding Officer's own residence, with facilities for visiting dignitaries as well. We had to do nothing, and we had to spend nothing either. There were six suites of rooms and a huge living area. A lady would come in the morning to cook our breakfast and in the meantime the icebox and cupboards were stacked with food and drink -particularly drink. "It's all yours", said Fred the manager. "Help yourselves". As if that was not ample hospitality, he told us that he had arranged to take us to dinner at a nearby roadhouse hotel; could we be ready in a couple of hours. We certainly could, and were collected by taxi and deposited at the hotel where we enjoyed a dinner of quality, washed down by wines of appropriate status, before being returned a bit the worse for wear to our sleeping quarters. We could only repay the compliment by taking Fred and his wife out to dinner the following evening. After a pleasant day looking around the locality we repaired to a high-class hotel restaurant with a high-class reputation and literally caroused the evening away - perhaps too well in my wife's case, for the next day she could not remember whether she had enjoyed the meal or not . I was in no doubt that I had done so.

The next leg of the trip was not too lengthy, but it involved a stop in Preston, where Nigel believed his roots to lie. We spent some time in the public library checking over census records and there was no doubt that this had been a family stronghold. We were making for Fleetwood, where Jill's family originated. Her brother had been born there, and her father was buried there. She had been evacuated there during the war, and many of her aunts, uncles and cousins were still to be found. The rest of the afternoon and evening were spent with some of these (to Nigel) long-lost relatives. Before retiring to rest in the famous North Euston Hotel, designed by Decimus Burton, we dined in a village a few miles away, where I won a pound by taking on a wager with one of Jill's cousins that I could not eat my way through the menu. I won, and to her credit she paid up.

The following day was a cross-country journey east across the Fylde, over the hills of the Forest of Bowland and on via Stonyhurst College to Settle. Things were going well and a minor problem on the way did not disturb our enjoyment. I was wearing clip-on sunglasses, and when I mounted to the roof of a stone watchtower on the top of the Pennines a howling wind took great glee in whipping them away and sending them sailing into the valley below. I considered this a small price to pay for the superb view and the no doubt salubrious fresh air. We arrived in Settle to find that most of the eating establishments were closed. Having found an excellent B&B place we enquired where we could eat. The landlady suggested the local fish and chip shop, which excited Nigel and Betty "I don't serve evening meals," she said, "but there will be a small supper waiting for you when you get back." The fish-and-chips, though eaten inside rather than out of the traditional and flavoursome newspaper, were magnificent, and after a stroll round the town we repaired to the guest-house ready for a good night's sleep. There was indeed a supper waiting for us. Why on earth did we bother to go out, we thought. There were sandwiches, rolls, cheese, cakes, buns and biscuits of many different types, with tea, coffee or cocoa to drink. It would have been discourteous not to do justice to this marvellous spread, so we did our best - which, though I say it myself, was not at all bad. We all slept heavily that night and awoke barely in time for a breakfast of similar size and variety. We forced ourselves, probably putting on pounds in the process. But who cares - we were on holiday and thoroughly enjoying it. We enjoyed it even more when we found how ridiculously small our bill was - undoubtedly the cheapest night on the whole of the trip, and not far off the best, either.

Next morning there were several beauty spots to visit - Malham Cove, Malham Tarn and the magnificent Gordale Scar; the longish walk to the latter was unanimously agreed to be well worth it. After a very, very good sandwich lunch at the Black Horse in Giggleswick, we set off again, mostly on 'B' roads, past Pen y Ghent and through Hawes to Kirkby Stephen; we were heading for the old market town of Appleby.There we met another set-back. There was some form of Fair on and there were no overnight vacancies in the town centre. On advice we tried one ex-Manor House off the Penrith road, but Jill and Betty, as accommodation inspectors-in-chief, were not satisfied. So we pushed on, hoping for better luck in Penrith. However, rounding a bend in the little village of Temple Sowerby, there was a hotel sign, at which we braked and turned in. The building was obviously three hundred years or more old - by the look of it a former manor farmhouse. Nigel and I waited in the car while the inspectors went to do their duty. We had hopes, but not too many. In five minutes the ladies reappeared. Taking one look at their faces and the spring in their step, Nigel said " We're in. It must be good". So we got out to hear the glad tidings that the main block was full but there was a converted coach-house, only recently finished, in which we could have two adjacent self-contained suites. Parking the car just outside, we entered one of the best-fitted hotel rooms I personally had ever seen. Even Nigel, a veteran of luxury hotels all round the world, was visibly impressed. Talk about falling on your feet, and the main block was equally good.

A comfortable lounge containing cabinets of Rockingham china; the gourmet restaurant habitually served at least five courses, each one adequate but not daunting in size; the service was impeccable and the wine list large and reasonably-priced. For two pins (not necessarily of beer) we would probably have cancelled the trip then and there and stayed on where we were; fortunately for our purses, the place was booked pretty solidly, so this was not an option.

After a breakfast which did not let down either the accommodation or the dinner, we went on our way, heading northwards to the Border country. By-passing Penrith, we stopped for coffee in the steeply-sloping market square at Alston before carrying on towards Haltwhistle and Hadrian's Wall. The latter really did impress both Betty and Nigel. Not surprising, when a house over one hundred years old in Canada tends to make people detour to have a look at it - or so Jill told me ; she had been but I hadn't. Then, ever pressing on to the north-east, we passed through Jedburgh and Kelso, and so eventually came to Coldstream. The guide book told us of a hotel actually on the Tweed, so we decided to try. This turned out to be huge Victorian Gothic house in its own extensive grounds, naturally with its own fishing. Fortunately the sport didn't interest us, but the end-product did when we found fresh-caught Tweed salmon on the dinner menu. Replete, we repaired to the basement bar. Nigel was a staunch Canadian Club man and tended to pooh-pooh the parent of all whiskey. But not for long. Having been persuaded to taste some of the top malts, he became an instant convert and declared his intention of baptising himself by sampling through the entire bar list. Even the announcement that the hotel stocked over one hundred different varieties did not deter him, but he didn't get far before he was haled off to bed by his anxious wife, obviously with an eye to the potential difficulties of the following morning.

We travelled zig-zag and quickly in the morning - a rapid on and off Holy Island, just beating the incoming tide across the causeway; through Alnwick with its magnificent Percy castle, and Alnmouth because I had once been sweet on the railway shedmaster's daughter there; a brief stop at the hydraulic history of Cragside; bypassing Durham via Quebec, as a compliment to Canada, and on to Barnard Castle, where the castle itself was outshone by the transplanted French chateau which now houses the Museum, amazing for the variety of its exhibits and for the low prices which their original collector paid for them. A few more miles took us on to Greta Bridge, to which once more we had been pointed by the guide book. Another bullseye for our Canadian cousins, who adored the semi-baronial atmosphere of oak furniture, coats-of-arms, sporting trophies and a huge, though unnecessary log-fire. After a good dinner Jill and I imbibed some

Canadian cultural ideas, especially in the shape of Betty's favourite post-prandial drink, creme-de-menthe frappe.

In the morning we began to feel that we were truly on the homeward leg of our trip. My feelings were mixed - I had thoroughly enjoyed the travelling which had taken in many places new to me, but I had to admit that my bank account was beginning to emit hollow sounds. Not far south we came to Richmond - another old stamping ground of mine. There, when in the army at Catterick, I had undergone my first real drunken evening, finishing up in the the cells for the night, fortunately under the auspices of a good friend who happened to be guard commander.

There were other, happier memories, as of the Great Ghost Hunt when with a party of friends I had set off on the last bus up Swaledale and disembarked miles from anywhere in order to test the truth of the legend of a phantom highwayman whose horse's hoofbeats could sometimes be heard reverberating across the top of the moors. We walked for miles, and thought we had struck pay dirt when our hair stood on end at the sound of drumming feet. Huddled together for protection, we watched a flock of startled sheep seeking pastures new. After sleeping in a chance hayloft, we returned to camp somewhat the worse for wear. I used to do a lot of walking in those dales, including my record day, achieved with a friend and with both of us wearing Army boots. We did thirty-six miles, up Swaledale, over the moors to Askrigg, and back down Wensleydale. At Askrigg, in a small Temperance hotel, I had enjoyed one of the most welcome meals of my life; though it was run a close second forty years later in Wales when, with Jill, I set out for a five-mile stroll, lost the way and did thirteen miles before stumbling into the only pub we had come across, just a couple of minutes before afternoon closing time. Beef sandwiches and Guinness have never tasted so good, believe me! The last memory of Richmond, apart from the castle and the view from it, was a street off the square where, in a small recording studio, the Catterick Jazz Band (including myself) had cut two sides and named one of them "Finkle Street Blues".

Our target was York. Leaving Richmond we followed as far as possible the route of my epic long walk, and came back down Wensleydale gasping for a drink. This was Theakston country, but we could not find a pub and it was nearly two o'clock. Eventually we screeched to a halt in Middleham with, apparently, a minute to spare. "Two pints and two halves of Old Peculier, please," we gasped to the barman. He proceeded in a leisurely fashion to the pump. "What's the hurry", he said; "we don't close till half-past." But we enjoyed it all the more.

After a brief pause at Masham to do homage to the home of Old Peculier we pushed on through Ripon and Harrogate towards York, looking forward to a good night and half the next day in that fine city.

But we reckoned without fate. As we approached the outskirts we started to try likely-looking establishments at which to stay. The answer was always the same - "Sorry! Full up". At last we found out why. It was race week. There being no point in hanging about hoping, we hurried past the fair city and kept our noses pointed south. By 6.30 we were getting a bit desperate, and were thankful to find accommodation in a large commercial hotel at Selby. Though it was by far the worst night we had spent since leaving home (even worse than the caravan), the management did their best and the other guests, commercial travellers to a man, were polite and friendly. When morning came, it brought with it a bonus after a near-disaster. We discovered the gem that is Selby Abbey. Though not religious I have always marvelled at the God-sent skills of the cathedral-builders. Ely is probably my favourite, though Wells is not far behind. But Selby was a real eye-opener, and it dazzled Betty. She could not see enough of it. So long did we spend there that we decided on a short hop that day and stopped at Lincoln, where we could see yet another magnificent building and, as it happened, enjoy some more fish and chips; we were in a B & B that night.

Leaving Lincoln, we went across the county towards the Wash. Passing through the flat indifference of the Fens we stopped momentarily at the wind-tunnel that is Kings Lynn and, after a cup of tea with my mother in Swaffham, visited the moated splendour of Oxburgh Hall, and then headed for Cambridge. It was a good job that we were not in a hurry. Having been delayed, not for the first time, by a herd of cattle anxious to get to the milking sheds, we turned a corner in a high-banked lane to see what looked like a heaving sea of dirty white and brown foam ahead of us. This was a first - a huge flock of sheep, milling in circles, trampling on each other, bleating furiously, scared stiff of our car yet urged relentlessly on past us by a half-dozen of busy, alert and occasionally snapping dogs. It seemed like half-an-hour before the road was clear, but it couldn't possibly have been that long. Relieved, we set off again, through the gentle Suffolk countryside and towards the shallow, rolling hills of North Essex. At Cambridge we halted for the last night, and in terms of problems it did not let us down.

We went straight to a new, five star hotel, full (by repute) of all modern conveniences and obviously planned to take advantage simultaneously of the burgeoning industrial areas around the town, its strong heritage-based tourism and the passing trade of University parents. It looked, probably by design, exclusive and expensive. We were shown to our rooms. Jill went into the bathroom and emitted a yelp of dismay. The room was wet and dirty, crumpled towels had been thrown all over the floor and the ash-tray was overflowing. If ever a complaint was justified, ours was, but although the damage was put right swiftly and competently, we felt that shrugged shoulders and a mumbled excuse about staff using the room to change was a less than adequate apology. But - it was the last night, so why spoil it. Mind you, we had our own back , though in a way which didn't say much for our intelligence. I tried to open the room window to clear the air a bit, and it promptly fell out. Presumably it was an early version of the windows which open up, down and sideways at one and the same time, but we had never seen one before. It took the maintenance man to fix it before we were able to get changed for what, at least, proved to be an enjoyable dinner.

Our last day started with the obligatory trip round the colleges, the town and the Backs. Betty was like a dog with two tails, and the coup de grace came with the organ playing and the choir singing in Henry VI's King's College Chapel. Her trip, at least, ended on a high note. We lunched before leaving and took the pretty way through Saffron Walden, Finchingfield, Thaxted and other typical North Essex villages and towns, arriving at our small flat overlooking the Isle of Dogs in time to change once more and go out for our very last meal of the tour.

There was no post-mortem to be held. Our holiday had ranged from the sublime to the ridiculous. There had been no hint whatsoever of discord amongst us; indeed we seemed to act like friends of twenty years rather than two days. Nigel and I each found in the other a mirror of his own dry humour, while Jill and Betty chatted incessantly in the back of the car, except when Betty was making notes or poring over the map. We fell naturally into the habit of paying our own overnight bills and covering other expenses out of a kitty, which Betty christened "The Dip". Each night we discussed plans for the next day, and Jill and I never failed to smile at Nigel's drawl whenever he wished to think about something - "I shall take that under advisement!" Perhaps it was fortunate that none of us had said that when the idea of the trip was first floated. Problems and mishaps notwithstanding, I personally had a very good time, and at least we didn't have a puncture the whole way.

THE STATUE

Neath mellow moon and searing sun he watches in the shaded square.
When I rest in oblivion he'll still be there.
He fears no peril, feels no pain of fragile flesh or brittle bone.
No rash emotions rack his brain of silent stone.
When children's chalks with ragged rhyme bedeck him on a holiday
he smiles, beneath his garish grime, to see them play.
The spirit of the place, he keeps his vigil as the children grow,
and when their sands run out, he weeps that they must go.
Neath melting moon and scorching sun he watches in the sheltered square.
When death and I and earth are one, he'll still be there.

Sir Robert Bingham-Palmer stands silently in Warrington Square. Or rather his statue does, for Sir Robert passed on a century ago to the land where children are not ill-treated, or exploited or abused. In death he enjoyed the unattainable Utopia of youth which for most of his life he had sought tirelessly to bring about. His was the grandest house in the square, though now it is virtually indistinguishable from the buildings round it, all having been first divided into apartments for the folk rather than for the fancy, and more recently converted to office use.

Sir Robert had no children of his own, but his house was staffed with kind, motherly women and was always open to waifs and strays who might otherwise have perished in fact, or in effect through disappearance into the vast underworld of venal cruelty which catered without shame or remorse for the worst vices of the rich. He particularly deplored two things in the nation's treatment of its children. The second of these was the exploitation of child labour in filthy conditions in the interest of profit, which in some cases simply fuelled the dreadful trade in young flesh. The first, and of equal importance to Sir Robert, was the total lack of education and upbringing of so many children of poor parents.

"How on earth", he used to say to his friends, "can we build a nation fit to rule the world if we do not provide proper training for future generations who must inevitably take up where we are obliged to leave off?" Sir Robert was nothing if not a supporter of Empire - the British one, of course.

When he died, Sir Robert Bingham-Palmer left a great deal of money to charities devoted to the ideals by which he had lived, a name revered by many people who, without his aid, might never have survived childhood, and a reputation which was preserved -spotless as it in fact was - in the social history books of succeeding generations. He also achieved the dignity of a statue of himself opposite the house in which his good works had been centred, and around this statue there grew up not long after his death a legend which reflected the absolute trust formerly placed in him.

Stated simply, the legend said that from time to time, in cases of serious danger to children in the locality, Sir Robert's statue came to life and intervened to save them. The reality of this is, of course, totally unlikely. But like so many legends which have gathered force for more than a century, the closer the examination of this one the more difficult it becomes to advance a merely prosaic explanation which might account for the reported facts - if indeed those facts are in essence to be relied upon.

The first report, within a year or two of Sir Robert's death, caused neither dramatic publicity nor even whispers among the residents of the Square. It was of an incident concerning the man (the word "gentleman" has deliberately been omitted) who had purchased the holy haven which Sir Robert had made of his home. This was a North London industrialist of the worst kind, who in his ruthless pursuit of profit recked not of human health and happiness (apart from his own) and cheerfully caused his workpeople to toil in conditions which even the most careless slave-owner in the West Indies might have considered too harsh. But then, slaves are to an extent an asset, and can breed other assets while the so-called free people of the slums of London were at that time totally as expendable as dogs and probably more so than monkeys, in whom some cost of training might have been invested. In confirmation of this assessment it is sufficient to advance just two words - "Match-girls".

Mr. Malachi Pettigrew was a thoroughly nasty man. He had a family of sorts, whom he treated almost as badly as his employees. He had already worn out and destroyed three wives and the fourth, after a mere five years of drudgery and insult, retained only strength enough to dream of vengeance. She had been a beauty, from a good family in poor circumstances which had accounted for her marriage to such a monster. She had borne her husband a daughter, now four years old, who inherited looks and disposition entirely from her mother's side. Little Lizzie Pettigrew was the darling of the ever-changing domestic staff of the great house, none of whom stayed for longer than they could help, with the sole exception of Butterton - valet, butler, secretary, general factotum, confidant and accomplice in evil of Mr Pettigrew. If that were considered possible, the man was even nastier than the master.

As Lizzie's mother began to sink rapidly into the same decline which had seen off her predecessors, the little girl found herself less and less with her mother and more and more with the household staff. Without exception that staff loved little Lizzie, for her beauty, her naturally winning ways, and the completely uncondescending manners which her mother had managed to teach her, by example as much as anything. In the house there were, however, two persons who were in different ways ambivalent in their attitude to the "little lady", as she was always called. Her father was prepared to bask in the glory of her presence on the very rare occasions when he entertained business associates; otherwise he ignored her altogether, and would have continued to do so until she was old enough to become some sort of marketable commodity or bargaining counter. Not so Butterton. Far from ignoring her, he coveted her in ways commensurate with the wickedness of his nature, yet hated her for her purity and innocence. One afternoon when Lizzie's mother was resting and most of the staff were busy preparing for one of the rare dinner parties, Lizzie sat playing sweetly by herself in the nursery between her bedroom and her mother's room, the suite being approached by a short flight of stairs. She found that a doll of which she was particularly fond was on a shelf out of her reach, and unthinking ran out of the nursery with the intention of seeking her mother's help. At that precise moment, Butterton was passing the door and she ran full tilt into his legs, causing him to stumble. "Ah, you would, would you, prissy little miss minx", snarled the valet and caught her a blow round the shoulders, so that she in her turn lost her balance and fell against him. The unexpected contact brought about a violent change in his face, which flushed darkly, accentuating the cruel, piglike eyes turned suddenly upon the little mortal at his feet. Pausing only momentarily to listen for any sound from the mother's room, Butterton fiercely grasped a plump, soft little arm and started to push the girl back into the nursery. The next thing he knew was a sensation of speed as he fell spreadeagled down the stairs and hit the floor below with a crack which served only to increase the pain already welling up from a contusion on his head. For a short time he lost consciousness, while Lizzie ran sobbing to her mother for comfort.

The mother, on hearing the little girl's story, resolved for her sake to brave the wrath of her husband on his return, and this she did to such effect that the valet received a tongue-lashing which made him cringe, as much as anything because he knew himself in the wrong. But that was all - he was far too useful to Mr Pettigrew, and knew far too much, to be dismissed. Nonetheless, the threat of future action was posed. Had Mr Pettigrew known it, this threat was unnecessary, as Butterton indicated when telling his story (suitably amended) to his cronies in the low public house which he frequented in his off-duty moments.

"I dunno wot 'appened", he said. "It was like runnin' 'ead on into a brick wall, and there was me rollin' backards dahn them dam stairs. And all I sore was that 'uge arm, like a lump o' stone." Charitably his mates assumed that he was a bit the worse for the fall and his subsequent intake of beer - at least until on the arm of the statue in the square appeared a small, red mark which soon faded in the rain.

And so began the legend of Sir Robert's statue.

On several occasions in the future, accidents to young children who rashly ran into the roadway round the Square were mysteriously averted, the drivers of the hansom cab, hackney carriage or motor vehicle piously attributing the escape to the Almighty or to providence. The children, however, thought differently and after the inevitable scolding from their worried but thankful parents talked of "the nice big man who picked me up and took me away from those horrible wheels". The length of time between incidents was usually long enough for memories of the previous occasion to have been half-forgotten, but there still lived in the Square old ladies who had known and feared Butterton and his master, and some even who had curtsied to Sir Robert as he cheerfully gave them "Good-day" on his swift and unassuming way about his philanthropic business. They knew, those old ladies. And so the legend acquired depth and strength, until most of the old residents of the Square would wave respectfully to Sir Robert as they passed by his statue, and did not neglect to teach their children and the children of more recent arrivals to do the same.

During the Great War the Square was not troubled much by the air-raids which hit other parts of London, but on one occasion while a warning was in effect, a small boy who was out much later than he should have been, and whose absence was causing considerable concern to his parents, was found sheltering between Sir Robert's legs. "He called me to take cover", the boy insisted, and this story did the legend no harm at all.

Things were different during the second great war, however, when death, fire and destruction rained from the skies on the long-suffering Londoners who (and in the Square this was most of them) had remained to defy the might of the German air-force. Some of the children had gone, of course, to safety in the heart of a countryside which they hated for its strangeness and its quiet, and because it was not their home. Those who stayed engaged in the usual war-time pursuits of young defiant Londoners - the gathering of shrapnel, fins of incendiary bombs, even the occasional fragment of aircraft. They spent their nights in uncomfortable air-raid shelters telling stories whose boastfulness increased in direct proportion to the seriousness of the raid in progress at the time. One or two collections of memorabilia included splinters of stone, for Sir Robert had not escaped a few direct hits from falling shrapnel and on one occasion the blast from a small bomb which had exploded at one side of the Square.

It was not until the dreadful V-weapons started to arrive that life became both dangerous and fraught with uncertainty. The V-1 was terrifying at first to the young children of the Square, with its horrendous high-pitched engine noise, its low flight path and its menacing tail of flame. But they quickly got used to these attacks and began to treat them with unwarranted disdain. Fortunately no flying-bomb fell closer than a quarter of a mile from the Square.
Then came worse - the suddenness and complete lack of warning of the V-2 rocket. Against this weapon there was no defence other than prayer or good-luck tokens and an impregnable shelter fifty feet below the ground - and even that was suspect. This phase of the war convinced any doubters among the residents of the Square of the utter truth of the legend of Sir Robert's statue. A houseful of children were engaged in a frugal birthday party at one corner of the square, when one of them looked out of the window and saw what appeared to be a swing suspended from Sir Robert's outstretched arm. "Hey! look at that", he shouted, and the entire crowd flooded out of the house, closely followed by parents and guardians, and surged across the Square towards the statue. When they arrived they looked up and saw nothing. "Must have been dirt on the window, you twit!" said his friend to the original instigator of the rush. But as the crowd turned to take up the party where they had left off, a massive thunder-crack came from the house which they had just quitted and it disappeared in smoke, flame and falling masonry and rubble. Awestruck, the children looked back at Sir Robert, and to their dying day not one of them ever deviated from the firm assertion that he appeared to be smiling.

The thankful parents were chastened and thoughtful as well as awestruck. The old ladies of the Square forbore not to point out that they had always supported the legend, and the incident even achieved minor press coverage at a time when news of all sorts competed fiercely for space in the shrunken newspapers. Even before the war had ended a residents' group was formed with the objective of renovating the somewhat dilapidated statue, and as soon as possible afterwards this worthy cause, well over-subscribed, was put into effect and a new plaque added to the plinth. Since that time there have been no more reported incidents to add to the legend, but that of course was unnecessary, so firmly had it become accepted and entrenched. Besides, children do not live in offices and play in areas devoted to car-parking, but curious clerical workers on their way to and from their places of employment can often be seen reading the legend about the legend:-

"In grateful memory of Sir Robert Bingham-Palmer,
who in life and in death kept faith with the children
of this Square".

TIME OUT OF JOINT

An uneasy peace lay over the whole of Western Europe. The flags, too, were troubled, stirring restlessly in small, furtive currents of air or hanging listlessly in resignation. Occasionally one would lift sufficiently to show in a top corner the emblem of Teutonia above the colours of the nation in which it was attempting to fly.

It was twenty years since the start of the hectic period of world-wide negotiation which had ended the last international war at the beginning of 1943. That crucial time had really commenced at the end of October 1942, when the then "German" armies had advanced deep into Russian territory and were within reach of the coveted oilfields just beyond. World history was diverted into a new phase when the nerve of the Russian leaders broke a few days too soon, before it had become obvious that the German advance had completely overreached itself. Russia sued for peace; Germany accepted, carefully not revealing the relief behind its assumed attitude of victor. The negotiations were brief, for Germany had expected to fight many more battles and was anxious to prevent a resumption of war on this particular front. So a treaty of future non-agression was signed, with deferred benefits to both sides to be effective as soon as the small matter of Germany's other opponents had been settled.

For Germany, the major benefits were to be the assimilation of parts of the small countries which divided it from Russia, this to be achieved by the partition of Poland, Hungary, Roumania and Jugoslavia. The sprat to catch the Russian sturgeon was the promise of a coastal corridor from the Black Sea through to the Mediterranean, with Albania and Greece thrown in, thus giving a substantial access to the Indian and Atlantic oceans , through either the Suez Canal or the Straits of Gibraltar. Finland was also added, almost as a makeweight, though it certainly wasn't Germany's to give.

With a deep, though inward, sigh of relief, Germany went off to pursue the war against England and its Commonwealth. Already there were signs that the United States were disenchanted with the whole affair. President Roosevelt in the last elections had defeated the Republicans under Wendell Wilkie by less than five million votes, and the furore of patriotic indignation sparked off by Pearl Harbour a year previously was beginning to wear off. The huge successes of the Japanese armed forces in conquering most of South East Asia in such a short space of time revived the cautious spirit of isolationism, and an increasing groundswell of opinion against war was making itself felt. The bombshell of a Russo-German pact, releasing Germany from at least half of its military commitment, destroyed the last bastions of the supporters of world involvement and America entered into talks with the Japanese government. At the same time, an approach was received from Australia and New Zealand with the idea of affiliation to the U.S.A. It took little time to settle with Japan; Anzania (as the new state was called) became a far-flung part of America, to be joined immediately and logically by Canada.

With an eye to future developments, approaches were also made to the various South American nations, and talks were set up to enquire into the possibility of a loose-knit federation taking in the whole of the American continent.

Japan was delighted to be relieved of a war of attrition with a country whose resources were far greater than its own, and within a year had assimilated the entire East Indies, Malaya, Burma, Siam and the Indian sub-continent. The Chinese republic, looking at this new Empire on its doorstep, took immediate steps to join Japan in a far-eastern power bloc. Thus, the world outside Europe was divided into three huge spheres of influence - Russia, Japan/China and America.

It did not take Germany long to polish off the remaining opposition from England, which had been left with only its fighting spirit when the flow of supplies from America ceased. At the very time when Germany was negotiating with Russia, the battle lines at El Alamein, the gateway between the Sahara desert and Egypt, erupted into a brief fury resulting in virtually no change in the dispositions of the opposing armies. The stalemate did not last long once the news of the other developments world-wide began to leak out. Germany, however, did not immediately over-run the Middle East. Aware of the alien, sometimes fanatical nature of the Moslem religion, the decision was taken to countenance a small Moslem block, self contained basically within Asia Minor and a small part of North Africa, which could serve two useful purposes. Germany firstly could see the benefit of a buffer between Europe and India, and secondly anticipated access to the Arab oilfields by supplying technology and through other trading activities. In due course, this came to pass more or less as planned.

Left completely out on a limb, England faced defeat and humiliation. This fate was mitigated by a totally unforeseen development within Germany. The already bloated ego of the German Fuehrer rose to such overbearing proportions that his generals could stomach it no longer. A carefully-laid plot, prepared on military lines and taking into account both the extent of the security with which the leader surrounded himself and the fanaticism of his still-loyal adherents, was put into effect and the body of Adolf Hitler was interred at his mountain fortress home with full honours and a plethora of tongue-in-cheek eulogies.

The way was clear to a negotiated settlement with England, a nation which, having been a frequent and valued ally, was still regarded as much closer to the Teutonic peoples than the neighbouring French. Besides, in France the legend of "Perfidious Albion" was still very much alive. After the architect of the victory of the Battle of Britain had chosen to die, by his own hand, in the spirit of devotion to his country which had inspired his last few years, a peace with at least a semblance of honour was concluded.

The talks between the victors and the many vanquished were protracted. Some of the conditions required by Germany were fought bitterly, and in some cases with success. The German generals respected the courage and spirit of the nations which had not only opposed them but come close to defeating them. The Treaty of Cologne, signed on 11th November 1943, changed the face of Europe, not so much by realignment of boundaries as by careful grouping of communities.

New sovereign states were set up, self-governing within the strict rules of a Western European Community whose head and fount of both rule and justice was Germany, now including all the partitioned lands to the East and Denmark and the Low Countries to the North-west. This expanded country was to be leader and master of Europe, under the new name Teutonia. France changed to Gallia, while Italy and its neighbouring islands - Sicily, Corsica and Sardinia, became Italia. Cunningly, Switzerland was to remain as a valuable international financial centre and meeting-place with the rest of the world.

The generals knew only too well the conspiratorial strengths which were inbuilt deep in the British character. The British Isles alone, therefore, found themselves divided into small units, while the rest of the Continent was grouped into much larger enclaves. Anglia, Scotia, Cambria and Hibernia became separate States. Neutral Sweden offered little opposition to the master-plan, and was merged with Norway to become Scandinavia, while Spain and Portugal together formed Hispania. Geographically the changes were not dramatic, but the small print contained many provisions which were not at all pleasing to the people at whom they were directed.

Firstly, the colonial nations, England, France and Belgium, were relieved of all responsibility for their African properties. In effect, the entire African continent with the exception of top and bottom fell into a new Teutonian Empire. The Sahara desert countries at the top were to join the Moslem bloc, and South

Africa at the bottom had no chance of holding aloof from subjection to the Empire. Its white population comforted itself with the thought that on past form Germans were not too likely to insist on equality for the coloured races whose country it had been in the first place.

Secondly, movement between countries was to be restricted to a bare minimum. Elaborate passport barriers and controls were instituted and strictly enforced with all the thoroughness of the disciplined nation which had been Germany. It may not have been designed to do so, but in fact this measure quickly solved the Irish problem by throwing North and South together within a restricted area. Each side had to acknowledge and adjust to the opinions of the other.

Movement control was not of itself onerous, but the ramifications of it stretched into facets which had far more serious implications. The official language of the entire Teutonian Empire was to be German. Existing native tongues were permitted to be spoken only within their established boundaries. Thus, travellers on business or other allowable activities were forced to learn either German or the language of the country which they proposed to visit. More cunning and more effective was the rule that all written correspondence which crossed a national boundary had to be in German, and a vast censorship machine was set up to enforce this.

The powers of self-government were small and restrictive, though a promise was made that these should be reviewed regularly for amendment in the light of experience. It has to be said also that some of the instructions applied equally to Germany itself. The population of Europe sighed and settled down to the normal occupation of trying to find ways by which the rules might be circumvented or at least bent.

Gradually, over the years, circumstances eased and things which had started as impositions became habits. Movement between countries was extended to a variety of activities including sport. This was predictable given the rise of the standard of and interest in football in Germany; here was an ideal way of underlining the superiority of the Teutonic races. One sport escalated into several. Hockey, tennis, athletics and swimming were added to the agenda. Cricket of course had continued in the closed environment in Anglia, and an audacious move by the M.C.C. was rewarded with success beyond all expectation. The game was selected, in part because of its reputation for gentlemanly fair play, for introduction to the other States within the Empire. This, of course, was always destined to be a slow and painful process because, apart from other considerations, of the essential Anglian characteristics of the game. After ten years, there were cricket clubs all over Europe and national sides were beginning to emerge. The overall standard of play was surprisingly high, the game being adapted by each nation to take best advantage of its own attributes. Thus, Teutonia became famous for its exponents of dogged defence; the batsmen of Gallia demonstrated the courage and dash (though sometimes also the volatility) of D'Artagnan and his colleagues; and from the height and physique of the Scandinavians many fast bowlers of great pace and accuracy were born. The inhabitants of the hotter climes of Hispania and Italia suffered, from the start, from the relative indolence which the heat of centuries had bred into their blood, but their guile was well-suited to the profession of spin-bowler, and in addition they proved willing to spend long hours virtually motionless in the position of Umpire, a function suited also to their ability to give decisions with all the facial appearance of conviction.

It was, therefore, a great occasion when a Teutonian Empire Cricket League was founded and regular annual matches were played for a trophy named, not after the erstwhile Ashes of English Cricket, but for a long-dead German general whose prowess and fair play on flat, sandy battle-fields was considered by his compatriots to have made him an ideal candidate for captaincy of a team upholding national honour on the no-less-flat green wicket of a cricket-ground. The first matches for the Rommel Cup were played to enormous crowds in stadia which only twenty years before had echoed to the stamping feet and shouted "Sieg Heils" of a previous and sadly misled generation of German youth. This fact was acknowledged by the sons of these men, who now felt it their necessary and important business to carry off the Rommel Cup against all comers and thus re-affirm their national superiority.
This view, naturally, had its mirror image in Anglia. The cricketing fraternity there turned single-mindedly to the task of winning the Rommel cup for their country, with the double objective of, primarily, assuaging the secret guilt of recent failure to reclaim from the now-Anzanian team the Ashes of a sport which, originated in England, had been taken up with such dedication and competence by expatriots. The second aim was to take revenge upon the Germany which had succeeded in inflicting upon them their first major national defeat in war for nearly a thousand years.
Joy was unconfined in Anglia when it became known that their team was to meet Teutonia in the final match to decide the winner of the jointly-coveted trophy. Newspaper columns of inordinate length and complexity discussed daily the pros and cons of the opposing teams, and in every inn (prohibition of public sale of [Teutonic] beer having been recently relaxed) bets were made, informed opinions voiced and forecasts ventured upon with never-failing optimism as to the eventual success of Anglia.

The match was to be played over five days, with the usual two innings for each team. The Anglian captain carefully watched the coin tossed by the chief umpire, and lost - mainly because he was unsure as to which side of the fifty-pfennig piece was heads and which was tails. Teutonia elected to bat first. With a dour Frieslander anchored stolidly at one end, the score mounted steadily, with a break for lunch, until two hundred runs were on the board for the loss of four wickets. Then the first Anglian change-bowler struck. Though erratic at most times, on his rare good days he was practically unplayable, and had been selected with some misgivings as to proportion of his good days to his bad ones. Three more wickets fell quickly for a handful of runs and the Teutonian tail, after attempting feebly to wag, left the field two hundred and sixty-two runs ahead. With thirty minutes of the first day's play left, the Anglian batsmen played cautiously. Too cautiously, as it happened, and a wicket fell in the penultimate over. Fortunately it was that of a night-watchman, but sixteen runs for one wicket did not look to be a brilliant start.

The next morning started with a sprinkling of rain, which slowed down the outfield but had not penetrated the wicket covers. The Teutonian bowling was disciplined and accurate, but not inspired, and the field placings seemed pedantic rather than boldly creative. The Anglian total increased in fits and starts, with a slow but steady scorer at one end and a hitter with a perfect eye and sense of timing at the other. At lunch no further wickets had been lost and the score stood at one hundred and twenty three for one. Within three overs afterwards, the situation had taken a turn very much for the worse. Two more wickets were down - one hundred and thirty six for three! At this point the Teutonic bowling tactics revealed a distinct lack of subtlety. The two latest wicket-takers were kept on and on until both of them had been virtually knocked off their length. Perhaps their reactions to consecutive boundaries left something to be desired; certainly they did not display the spirit which often led an Anglian bowler to dangle a scoring opportunity as bait before producing a perfectly-judged and to all appearances identical ball which beat the bat but not the stumps. Just before tea another wicket fell, to a marginal l.b.w. decision.
The incoming batsman attempted to loft his first delivery over long on for six, but unfortunately simply directed the ball into the huge waiting hands of the dour Freieslander. The score was one hundred and ninety eight for five. After the break both new batsman and old decided to dig in and the run rate dropped to a mere trickle. Nonetheless, the two were still together at close of play; two hundred and thirty eight for five.

On the following day there was again some rain, and play did not start until early afternoon, when a watery sun had appeared through the low passing clouds. The Teutonic bowlers redoubled their efforts, literally steaming in at great velocity as though determined to remove the offending stumps at the other end in one gigantic flight to the boundary. While not achieving that particular objective they did succeed in removing two more batsmen before the tea-break, but not without seeing quite a few added to the score mounting on the new high-tech board which had been proudly introduced as a product of Teutonic ingenuity. Two hundred and eighty six for seven, a lead of twenty four runs with three wickets standing. After the break, the scoring went on slowly but the advantage of the massive hands of most of the Teutonic fielders made itself felt, in that not even the slimmest chance of a catch was ever missed, and two brilliant takes in the slips, followed by a displaced middle-stump, saw the end of the Anglian first innings at three hundred and twenty runs: - fifty eight runs ahead.

Try as they might, the Anglian bowlers failed to dismiss the Frieslander and his equally obstructive partner from halfway down the batting order, and the third day closed with the Teutonians well on the way to wiping out the deficit. Thirty three for no wicket.

The fourth day dawned fine and warm, and the wicket looked a batsman's paradise. This indeed was how the Teutonian team treated it. Having regained the lead without loss, by lunch they had scored just over a hundred runs, with the score at one hundred and forty for one. It is doubtful whether over-confidence actually encouraged over-eating, but there was a definite change in the scoring rate in the afternoon session. Not only did the run rate itself drop, but the fluidity of the morning's stroke-play seemed seemed to have suffered a relapse. Encouraged, the Anglian bowlers redoubled their efforts, urged on by some cunning tactical changes engineered by their captain. Wickets began to fall. At tea it was two hundred and six for five wickets, and Teutonia were one hundred and forty eight ahead. A collapse immediately on resumption of play saw two more wickets go down, but at the close the score was one hundred and ninety nine for seven.

On the next and last day day, another fine one, the morning opened with some spectacular scoring by a giant Teuton known more for his bowling. He added forty runs before being caught on the square leg boundary. After his departure it did not take long for the Anglian team to see off the remaining two batsmen, unfortunately leaving the necessity for their own second innings to be opened before lunch. Their opponents' score of two hundred and seventy nine left them needing two hundred and twenty two in approximately four and a quarter hours;

the match was scheduled to end promptly at six p.m.and Teutonic clocks were noted for their accurate timekeeping. The twenty minutes before lunch saw fierce attacking bowling from the Teutonians, and equally determined defence from the Anglian openers. No wickets down but only twelve runs on the board. The required run rate had risen to fifty five an hour - practically a run a minute. Over lunch the Anglian captain had a word with the natural hitter who had scored a half century in the first innings, and his more polished and stylish partner. " You've got to stick there at all costs, Charlie", he said to the latter; "As for you, Bill, go for it, but carefully. If you can get three figures on the board in an hour and a half, we're in with a chance." The innings resumed. The batsmen obeyed to the letter their skipper's instructions. In an hour and a quarter, Charlie himself scored only seventeen runs, but Bill laid about the bowlers as though they were Sunday cricketers on a village green. His fifty came up within the hour, and he continued in the same vein until, at eighty eight, he tried a hook-shot once too often, mis-cued and was caught easily behind the wicket. One hundred and twenty six for one; ninety six more needed for victory.

With thirty minutes to go before tea, the skipper sent in another potential hitter from lower down the order rather than a more recognised batsman. It did not work. Charlie kept up his end in his normal quiet and efficent manner, occasionally farming the bowling if he thought his partner needed a break, but before tea he saw two further wickets fall at the other end with just twenty more runs on the board. At tea the score stood at one hundred and forty six for three; seventy six needed in under two hours.
A situation on the verge of desperation needed a desperate remedy. "Keep it up, Charlie", his captain ordered; " The one thing we can't afford is to lose you now." Play resumed, as did the normal batting order, but the electric sense of urgency was communicating itself to both teams. Incoming batsmen were told to take whatever chances they thought justified, and the Teutonic bowlers rolled up their sleeves, gnashed their teeth and contorted their large faces into the semblance of angry, man-eating giants. The duel was a great spectacle, and no-one lucky enough to have one of the well-oversubscribed seats that day will ever forget it. By five o'clock, just twenty five runs had been added, for the loss of two wickets. Five more to fall, and fifty one runs needed in one hour. The skipper changed tactics again. The next two batsmen sent in were not even hitters. They were in the side exclusively for their bowling ability, but as such they had good eyes for a ball, and broad shoulders. The skipper did not mince his words. "Just go in and slog", he ordered. For twenty minutes, this worked well. At the end of this time the score was one hundred and ninety four for seven. Three wickets to play with and another twenty eight runs needed.

Saving until last the batsmen highest up the order, the captain sent in another bowler who had to his credit some slight success with the bat, though mainly by way of defence. The scoring rate dropped again. With twenty five minutes to go, still three wickets in hand, and seventeen runs away from victory, the skipper signalled to Charlie to break the mould. The field was a classic model of the Teutonic idea of defence. Not a gap to be seen around the batsman's end, and just three out fielders to attempt to stop any stroke which dared to penetrate the inner ring. Charlie surveyed the placings carefully.. His eye was well in, and he had had a good look at all the bowlers. He settled down on strike. The first ball would have done credit to Harold Larwood at his fastest, and he watched it carefully past his off stump. The next was slower, straighter and more fully pitched. Charlie's eye never left it as he picked it neatly off his toes and directed it with care between short leg and mid-on. But he reckoned without the athletic ability of short leg, who leapt to his left and flung out a huge hand to which the ball stuck as if by a miracle. Charlie stood as if mesmerised before shaking his head sadly and starting on the long, lonely walk back to the pavilion. Two more wickets left.

Next in was a Yorkshireman, an all-rounder of vast experience and nerves like steel. He took strike, glared intimidatingly at the bowler and promptly dispatched the next ball to the boundary over the head of extra cover. Thirteen needed. Unlucky for some, thought the skipper, his hands and his brow running with perspiration. No further score that over. Thirteen to get in nineteen minutes.

At the other end the defending batsman steeled himself. Two deliveries he ignored. The third he blocked, but the fourth was a poor one and he swung it easily away over the inner ring of fielders to the onside boundary, where the failsafe man just failed to stop it. Nine more to go. Nothing more off that over, and the Teutonian captain showed some unexpected guile by changing to a medium pacer of well-known accuracy and consistency. A maiden over resulted. Twelve minutes left.

The next over was a repeat of the previous one at that end. One gigantic four and nothing off the rest. Five runs wanted in seven minutes. Again the accuracy merchant facing the burly Yorkshireman, and again a maiden. Now only four minutes remained and still five runs were needed. It was almost certain that the next over would be the last. It started. First ball, no score. Then a slashed two along the ground through the covers. Four balls, and three runs. The third, fourth and fifth deliveries were dead straight and of perfect length. No chance of scoring without risk, even though there would be another wicket remaining. The tension was unbearable as the tall blond Teuton approached the bowling crease at speed and threw down the last ball of the match. The batsman took a deep breath and a firm grip on his bat. It was a good though not a great delivery, and it was pushed away past mid-on, where there was some distance to the sparse outer ring. The batsmen galloped the first run and turned for a second. It was touch and go, but the run would mean a drawn match. They tried it. Long-on gathered the ball in his stride and threw it deftly at the bowler's end. The incoming batsman strained every muscle to get his bat down behind the crease, but the bowler fumbled the ball, and here his lack of the ingrained experience of many years which was part of the Anglian team's heritage betrayed him. Cursing at himself, he noted quickly that the runner at the other end was still out of his crease there. He hurled the ball at the opposite stumps, but in his desperate haste his aim was just sufficently inaccurate to miss not only the wicket but the oustretched glove of the wicket-keeper. There was a great shout from the batsman who had turned at the other end. "Come on! One more". By the time the overthrown ball had been returned to the keeper, both batsmen were safe home and Anglia had won by two wickets.

Inexperienced though they possibly were in some of the finer points of the ancient game, the Teutons were at root gentlemen, and sportsmen. Without exception or hesitation they gathered round the batsmen, offering their congratulations. For the whole of the next week Anglia was in ecstatic uproar. To turn a trite phrase on its head, they may have lost the old war but they had won the new battle, and national pride could be restored to the heart and mind of every single inhabitant of the little island of Anglia. In both countries the press was full of ball-by-ball accounts of the game, and stirring commendations of the spirit in which it was played. "This match", said the leader in 'The Times', "has done more to restore a friendly relationship between our two nations than might have been achieved by another twenty years of trying to forget."

The two umpires appointed to oversee the match came, respectively from Turin and Lisbon. Back in their own countries each gave an exclusive interview to his own press. "This shows", declared the Italian, " that a firm Mediterranean hand can act as a force for the imposition of the rule of reason." The Portuguese (for so he still regarded himself) put it more simply. "It was no more than it should have been," he said. "the Teutonian team had to be defeated. I actually called 'No-ball!' when the winning stroke was played, but nobody took any notice."

LIFE MUST GO ON

I lay on my own side of the bed - the right-hand side, where I had always lain for nearly fifty years. I listened for the sound of gentle breathing, or of soft snoring or the occasional heavy snort, but heard nothing, not even the muffled jumble of sleep-talking. I stretched out my arm across the bed, but encountered only emptiness and desolation.

As if looking at one of the classic films in my videotape collection, I watched myself reliving recent events. The telephone call - "She's in hospital - collapsed while playing carpet bowls". This was an activity which she enjoyed, for the company, the gentle exercise and the off-chance of winning. After more than half a lifetime together it is best to spend some time apart, each doing things which the other does not particularly want to do.

Then the dash to the hospital, to find a stranger in a bed with my wife's name on it; a shell of a woman, with grey and sagging features and bristling with wires and tubes. The children arriving posthaste, shocked and incredulous, but unfortunately in time to take away a picture of their mother which would haunt them for ever. I always feel that the dead should be remembered at their best, but I suppose somebody has to face the worst.

The end - imperceptible because it had really taken place hours before. The trauma of making arrangements to satisfy both decency and bureaucracy, and the heartbreak of removing personal memories in order to avoid further pain. The hollowness of the mandatory meeting in the crematorium chapel, with well-meaning people trying to help but only making loss still more difficult to bear. And standing in the front pew with our children beside me, feeling a hundred eyes on my back like kindly dagger thrusts I understood how, on the occasions when I was merely in attendance at such functions, the feeling of sympathy, however deep, had always been tempered by the thought "Thank God it's not my turn yet".

But that was the easy part. The so-called wake was more difficult, parrying constant expressions of condolence, respect and encouragement. Why is it called "a wake", when everybody knows damned well that death is a permanent sleep for the departed and an ongoing nightmare for those left behind? I had few friends, while she had had many. I knew, though, that all of them were real friends and felt sincerely for me. But at the moment I could not think straight; instead I felt anger that I was the one with the loss, and jealousy that some of them, at least, were still paired. Now, in bed alone, I had to face the future when I was not sure that it even existed for me.

The videotape hummed on, taking me back through my life, as we are always told happens to a drowning man. I never knew either why I married her, or why she married me. I suppose that, having always been shy and burdened with a huge inferiority complex, I was dazzled by anyone prepared to go out with me. That was simple, but why did a pretty, vivacious girl with a boy-friend for every day of the year take any notice of me? A whirlwind courtship and a short engagement ended in a marriage which evoked prophecies of disaster from some of her relatives. My upbringing certainly had not left me lacking in physical desire, and that was probably part of the equation. But we were both virgins on our marriage night, and not for lack of either inclination or opportunity. Perhaps this was a logical manifestation of a Victorian emotional legacy.

That was forty-six years ago, and forty-six years of thick and thin - largely thin, because we started with nothing and I was too busy being ambitious for success to realise that what I should really have been seeking was the maturity which did not arrive until I was of retirement age. Still, we stuck together and raised two children who of recent years had found time to support us as good friends rather than just family. By just caring for them and always being there in time of their need, our unwittingly-sown seeds flowered and bore a rich harvest.
Mind you, there were times when our marriage was touch and go; probably this is normal. In my case I had to contend with the background of an inherited emotional block. In my family it was a weakness to show emotion. Until now I found it difficult to use the word "love" in a connotation stronger that that applied to such pleaures as food and drink. The stiff-upper-lip syndrome was a religion whose high-priest was my mother's father, and even my much-more-human stepfather was repressed by it. But he brought me up as his own son, and for this I regarded him with a respect born of liking and gratitude. I realised then that I had withheld from the person who above all should have received it the simple gift of the expression of love. I had always been ready and pleased to give material things, but I had never really told her unequivocally that I loved her.

As I lay there stupified by misery, I remembered also my guilt in failing to consider her as a partner rather than some sort of super-employee, in not understanding her feelings, and, in effect, in displaying an unjustified and overweening selfishness by putting my own interests first. Perhaps the fact that for several years I habitually left her to look after the children alone while I pursued my hobby of jazz might be part-justified by the fact that I did earn a bit of extra money. But I was usually generous with money when I could afford it, when what she really wanted was love, and that would have cost me nothing beyond a realisation of the stupidity of my repressed emotional outlook.

Small wonder that I drove her into a situation where she was tempted to find elsewhere those things which I did not give her. Once, by the chance discovery of a letter, I was devastated by the realisation of what I had done - or, rather, not done. For many years she found great pleasure in amateur operatics, where her youthful looks and excellent singing voice put her in demand for leading parts in a certain type of show. I supported her by going to the shows, but never enjoyed the - to me distasteful and forced - larger-than-life atmosphere engendered by a group of people whose hobby involved playing a part, or being someone different. That attitude now seemed sheer arrogance. The inevitable happened, and an apparent romance emerged, no doubt helped by the fact that by that time some of her leading men were little older than our son. Serious thought convinced me that the basic blame rested with me, and I offered to make things easy for her. At the same time, I was jolted into a realisation that I did not want her to go, and I tried to make this plain. Anyway, she stayed, and from then on we were a lot closer, though probably still subnormally so far as I was concerned. But I had learned to appreciate things which previously I had either just not considered or taken for granted. And I found myself watching her movements, wanting to touch her softness, and marvelling that, despite everything, she was mine. Importantly, too, I found that I could be moved by both joy and sadness in a book or film. But I still had not completely conquered my inhibitions.

As more years went by, my good fortune became evident when my business failed and only her support and (paradoxically) her toughness kept me alive at a time when I could not look over a parapet and had to keep my back pressed to the tiles of Underground platforms. In our years of retirement we had spent only a handful of nights apart, and had built a happy life in which we did many things together but still retained individual interests.

For fifty-five years I had occasionally written scraps of verse - amateurish poetry which pleased me, especially when it attempted to embody the spirit of jazz. Unbidden into my head there now came a simple, classic blues which I had polished until its hopelessness shone like the moon in black night, and called "Grey Dawn Blues".

Grey light of morning stood silent by my bed;
grey thoughts were dawning, sadness weighed my head.
Nobody told me, but I knew my girl was dead.
Three words of comfort laid her in the ground;
three snow-white roses on a bare earth mound;
Just can't believe my girl won't be around.
Red sky at morning, purple sky at night;
yellow her picture in the candlelight;
all turn to shadow; colours don't seem right.
Going to the river and its mud-brown tide.
Can't stand my sorrow, got no place to hide.
No need for living since my baby died.

As my searching hand found no soft, answering pressure, the full realisation came to me. She was gone, and I was alone. The tears came then, but even as they crept down my cheeks I knew that they were not for her, but mainly for myself. As though in sympathy with the dampness of my eyes, I needed to go to the bathroom. On the window-ledge was a brown bottle of pain-killers, which I rarely took, but which seemed to help the small aches and pains which she frequently suffered - pulled muscles, neuralgia, and the usual problems which beset an ageing body. No more than a handful of tablets remained. On an impulse I tipped them into my palm, ran a glass of water and swallowed them deliberately, one by one. Perhaps I knew that there were not enough to do any serious damage, but the pain was twisting me in knots and by now the tears were falling fast enough to fill the glass themselves. I went back to bed and must have cried myself to sleep.

Somewhere a bell was ringing. My consciousness struggled up through oceans of wet cotton wool and emerged into daylight. I picked up the phone. It was my son who, having inherited not a little of his mother's toughness, had done well in business and owned one or two properties round and about. Our clan households - son's, daughter's and ours - were situated in an almost exact geographical equilateral triangle, with each side 150 miles long. "Look, Dad,", he said, " we've been thinking. One of my flats down here is empty. Would you like to take it? At least you'll be a bit closer to us. Mull it over, and let me know".
As I replaced the receiver, I noticed that the pillows on her side of the bed were undented, and the bedclothes relatively tidy - not the usual twisted and tumbled heap. I went downstairs and without thinking switched on the CD player. I listened to two of her favourite tracks - Louis Armstrong's "I want a little girl",

and George Thomas with McKinney's Cotton Pickers, singing "If I could be with you one hour tonight". I didn't cry.

So somehow I knew that the worst was over. This was how she would have wanted it. This was how I would have wanted it had the situation been reversed. All the trite things I had ever heard or read about death and bereavement suddenly acquired meaning. Remember the good times. Life is for the living. When one door closes, another opens. Life, I realised, must go on. There were books to be read and hopefully books to be written. Music to be played and wine to be enjoyed. My small grand-daughter, who trusted and loved me, to be cherished. It would take time to adjust outwardly, but always there would be my private memories, bright behind a locked door.

I passed into the sunshine of the kitchen and began to get my breakfast.

STOP ME AND BUY ONE

In the days before the " War which nearly destroyed the World ", childhood was very much different from today's frenzy of television violence and sex. It still had its dangers, but these were less common and still less publicised. Nonetheless, to be under ten years old in 1938 was to have lived in an era which was soon to vanish like snow beneath the sun. Children were not expected to be streetwise and thus retained their innocence into their teen years, protected by the prevalent standards of normal behaviour and in a last resort by 99% of their elders.

Those were the days when children approaching the end of their first decade could go on their own to their local recreation ground, play with their friends on the swings or at some boisterous ball game, and return home safely - preferably by the time specified by their parents, because otherwise the privilege might be withdrawn. Mysterious play-seasons came and went as though at the command of a football referee's whistle. Out of the blue a whispered word seemed to be broadcast over the airwaves, and tops were summarily put away, to be replaced by hoops; or, with the advent of April showers, skipping or hopscotch might give way overnight to the absorbing pastime of racing spent matchsticks down the brimming gutters. This could be done quite safely, for there was little traffic in the residential streets, and what there was did not travel very quickly.

On the sunny afternoons of summer weekends, it was the turn of the parents, and whole families would repair to the local tennis-club, where some of the grown-ups played a strenuous form of lawn-tennis, while others contented themselves with the gentler practice of pat-ball. But they were in the fashion, which meant a great deal to the middle class of the 1930s. Meanwhile, the children would attempt weird ball and stick games of their own invention, or play hide-and-seek round the clubhouse with occasional breaks for the consumption of sickly yellow lemonade made from equally dubious-looking powder. Then, of course, there were ice- creams. At the sound of a jangling, louder-than-usual bicycle bell, games would stop, parents would be mobbed to disgorge pennies, and a howling mob of youngsters would set off in pursuit of the tinkling music. If they were served at the very gates of the club, so much the better; but if not, they had a certain latitude to traverse a street or two under the supervision of the oldest among them until they caught up with the source of the magic sound.

This was a peculiar-looking vehicle, with at the front two bicycle-wheels supporting a large almost square box, and at the rear a third wheel on which, on a large and apparently uncomfortable saddle sat the Ice-Cream Man, resplendent in coat, apron and cap in the colours of his particular brand of confection. He guided his clumsy steed by means of a straight bar attached to the rear end of the box and bearing the most important instrument of his calling - the BELL. Emblazoned on the sides of this box-tricycle were pictures of the delicacies for sale, and always the legend from which minor differences in taste, size or quality might be ascertained by the cognoscenti. Be it Walls, or Lyons, or Eldorado, the children formed immutable preferences and were known on occasion to turn round and return empty-handed to their parents because "it wasn't the one I like". For one penny, five minutes of freezing stickiness could be obtained, in the shape of a triangular, open-ended cardboard packet in which nestled, like a funnel-spider in its lair, a Snofrute, or (better still) a Snocreme - the first being pure water ice and the second exactly what its name suggested. Furthermore, some accommodating salesmen were not above dividing one of these eskimo delights into two parts and selling each for one halfpenny.

One such of these salesmen resided and traded in a northern town. His stock in trade was purchased wholesale, and his banner read "MR. SID". Not for him the ignominy of employment. He was Principal of his own retail empire, and woe betide the child who failed to acknowledge this fact. A protocol had to be observed. There was no "Hey, mister, have you got any chocolate flavour?". Enquiries and requests for service must be formally addressed, and prefaced by the magic words "Please, Mr. Sid".
It is not certain what happened, or even when or why exactly it happened, but Mr.Sid acquired a deep secret. Perhaps it came to him suddenly, possibly it was the maturing of an inherited gene, or perhaps constant contact with his infant customers gave him ideas above and beyond the norm of retailer/customer relations. But it came, not perceptibly but more suddenly, in an urge to get to know his little buyers more intimately.

Now, Mr.Sid was nobody's fool. He quickly perceived the direction in which his thoughts were taking him, and decided that if he was to extend his fancies into fact he must do so according to a meticulous and foolproof plan. He was unmarried, had no real friends, and his parents were long dead. So he gave out that he was moving to a distant part of the country, bought a plain van large enough to hold his tricycle, fitted it with a folding ramp to facilitate quick loading and unloading, and left without leaving a forwarding address. He also bought a supply of paint carefully matched to the colours used by his competitors in business. After a short holiday, during which he perfected his plan of campaign, Mr. Sid, with some reluctance, effaced his identity from his tricycle and fitted a cunning system of boards which, painted in the appropriate livery, could change his apparent business allegiance. He also acquired an up-to-date list of the wholesale and retail outlets of all the manufacturers whose henchmen he intended to impersonate.

For a while, Mr.Sid traded with complete propriety. As much of his business was in holiday areas, he stayed at bed and breakfast establishments, bought his stock as soon as the wholesalers opened each day, and resold it in the streets to casual customers. He did, however, institute certain different practices as part of his trading methods. First, the name "Sid" never again passed his lips or appeared in his mobile advertising material. Second, he took great trouble to find out the normal routes and timing favoured by the salesmen employed by the firm which he had chosen as the recipient of his custom, and great care not in any way to clash with them. And thirdly he began to work up a sort of sales patter calculated to attract his demanding but still naive customers. For instance, he would offer prizes for answering simple educational questions, the prizes being either free merchandise or a ride on his tricycle. The ride was graduated as to on the box or on the saddle, and by time according to the difficulty of the question posed. These business methods quickly made him popular wherever he went - and he rarely stayed more than a couple of days in any one place. During this initial period of adjustment he observed more closely his quarry - for hunter he now was - and their likes and dislikes, strengths and vulnerabilities, and in particular their responses to his various sales ploys.

Eventually, he felt that he was ready to put into operation the full range of his plan. To him, this was indeed a master-plan, but to the world at large, had they known of its existence, it would have been a concept of the utmost degradation, an affront against decency, and an offence punishable not merely by death but by the most lingering and painful death which the ingenuity of man could devise. Of all this Mr.Sid was probably well aware and probably equally dismissive. His inclination had become an obsession, and his obsession was of the most horrible kind. He was now one of the monsters who prey sexually upon young children. His catholic taste - boys or girls were acceptable - was no mitigating factor; even he accepted that. But an obsession demanded satisfaction, and in a few English towns, north, south, east and west of Watford Gap, mysterious disappearances of young children began to occur. There were never two occurrences in the same town; there was no pattern in the sex of the missing children, or in their appearance, age or clothing. They just vanished from the earth and not once was a body recovered. Mr. Sid was too clever for that.

His method, refined by practice, consisted of a simple step by step procedure. The innocent question game, after initial consumption of ice-cream. The prize choice, in which the winner was always persuaded to accept the ride on the tricycle; a leisurely journey to a quiet spot nearby, always well chosen in advance, and finally a light tap on a curly (or other) head, followed by a swift disposal of a small body in the secret, refrigerated chamber which Mr. Sid had painstakingly converted from normal ice-cream storage space. This compartment was large enough to accommodate (in folded-up form) a nine-year-old child of average size. The details of the fate and subsequent disposal of these tiny, innocent unfortunates will never be known, and would, in any case, probably be of such horror as to defy description.

It was fortunate that before more than a handful of towns had been traumatised by this inexplicable culling of their future citizens, there occurred two events which, had Mr.Sid been less pleased with his own ingenuity, he might reasonably have foreseen. Firstly, a properly accredited representative of the ice-cream firm which was at the time unwittingly providing him with cover happened to run across Mr.Sid in the street and, having given chase unsuccessfully, reported his experience to his supervisor. Shortly afterwards, careful questioning of some of the companions of the missing children elicted facts which had not previously emerged, but which pointed unmistakeably to a tricyclised ice-cream vendor as a likely candidate for investigation.

The machinery of justice swung into action, for this type of crime ranks very high in its undesirability. Back records in other towns were swiftly checked, and soon confirmed the suspicions being voiced. Despite the preference of the police for an undercover operation, in fairness to all parents a massive Press campaign was mounted, stating the facts and urging vigilance of the highest order. And ice-cream sales from mobile shops plummetted, soon bringing about decisions to cut back or drop altogether this type of selling. Great banner headlines appeared in all newspapers, national and local, leading and struggling, daily and weekly. Mr. Sid, though anonymous under various trading names, became notorious as "The Pedalling Paedophile", and was quickly forced to abandon his carefully- prepared modus operandi. But his addiction was now stronger and his need greater. Unwisely he attempted another exercise in an area which he thought still safe for him. But he reckoned without the ingrained horror felt by the population at large when confronted with his loathsome activities, and having got as far as the capture of the unfortunate infant who was destined to be his last victim, was chased by a growing crowd and only managed to escape by his fall-back knowledge of the neigbourhood concerned. Just managing to keep ahead of his pursuers, he bundled his tricycle into his van and drove off furiously out of the town.

The end came quickly. Rounding far too rapidly a bend above a quarry, Mr.Sid lost control of the van and he, van, tricycle and his mercifully unconscious final victim plunged eighty feet to the water below, which was deep enough to prevent total disintegration but not so deep as to make recovery difficult. Mr.Sid was dead, almost cut in two; his tricycle, battered but recognisable, was pulled from the wreckage of the van and with it the sad but undefiled body of the last winner of his heinous prize. It was as well that the final gruesome detail was not allowed to be made public; of course, Mr.Sid's name was already anathema. The converted freezing compartment at first puzzled the investigators as to its purpose, but this became horribly clear from the discovery of a drawer containing a small syringe and a supply of a drug of which a minute injection would bring about a quick and painless death. Mr.Sid may have been a necrophiliac, but he was no sadist.

THE CASE OF THE MISSING MARBLE

Hatchington Hall, that famous stately home, was in a state of uproar. As is well-known, the magnificent collections now on display to the public were accumulated over several centuries by successive members of a family which combined wealth with the appreciation of works of art. What may not be quite so well understood is that not one of these collectors knew a great deal about what he or she was accumulating. But they all possessed, in addition to a magpie complex, an instinctive flair for beauty and a good idea of the relative importance of rarity, artistic merit, and value for money. And for two hundred years nothing had been sold, not even for death duties. There was not a museum in the world which did not covet this conglomeration of fine art and ephemera gathered under the one roof. The way in which the collections were scattered throughout the house without any attempt at segregation of like with like was the envy of every other great house with similar pretensions. Thus, one could spend an hour in just a single room without plumbing the depths of the ocean of beauty, value and historical association washing gently and nonchalantly against the four walls which contained it. The house was one incredible surprise, from top to bottom.

The uproar taking place at this particular time was caused by an unprecedented event. Although this was before the time of closed circuit television, pressure pads, alarms and tiny electric wiring, never before had an attempt been made in broad daylight to steal a single one of the treasures on display. One or two potential break-ins at night had been thwarted by the vigilance of a dedicated security staff, and their daytime counterparts had a pretty good system going which had kept the treasures safe during visiting hours. Until now, that is. Hitherto, apparently, the awe and appreciation of the fact that such a priceless collection was available to public view had engendered a protective attitude on the part of the public.

Now, in one of the great drawing-rooms, George Bidgood, the duty guide, had pressed the emergency button, something which had rarely happened except for test purposes. On finishing his current one-hour stint, George had carried out his usual visual check. Stepping over the red cord which marked the limits of public access, he went straight to a black plinth on which should have stood one of the greatest treasures of the house - a marble figure of a small putto, executed by the great Michelangelo in about 1510. Sure enough, it had gone and had been replaced by a cheap plaster Cupid , while on the floor in front of it was a crude notice which had obviously been hung from the figure's neck but had since fallen to the floor. "The original of this piece has been removed temporarily for conservation," read the card. George leapt back to his post and pushed the panic button, which meant that everyone within the house had to remain there for the time being, and no further visitors were admitted.

By this time his relief had arrived. The police would be there within fifteen minutes, but meanwhile the curatorial staff were busy examining bags and packages, most of which in accordance with the rules had been left at reception. They found nothing untoward. Shocked faces continued to file past George's post by the exit door to the room, having gasped incredulously at the empty plinth. "How could it have been done?" they asked among themselves, and "Who could possibly have done it?

Among those passing were a boy of some fourteen years and a little old man, obviously an eccentric, with bright eyes and a straggly beard. In a shrill, bird-like voice, the old man addressed George and his colleagues, various of whom including the curator in charge had now gathered in the bereaved room. "Have no fear", he said, "Help is here. This (pointing to the boy) is my nephew Charley Barnes, the celebrated boy-detective who has recently solved several crimes which had baffled the police force. I am his assistant as well as his uncle. Just what is the problem?"

It was perhaps incongrous that help from such an unexpected and unconventional quarter should be readily accepted, but the Curator in the circumstances would have clutched at a lifeline held out by the Devil himself. With George's help he explained what had happened. "Must have been several of them, Unk", Charley opined; "One to distract, one to lift and one to carry." "You mean an organised gang?", returned his uncle. "Correct", replied Charley, "and we know a bit about gangs, don't we, after our last success." " Of course", said the little man. "You mean the group of roughs who let off a case of dynamite in that actress's bedroom?" "Right", affirmed Charley, " The Case of the Gang Bang". A few of the bystanders sniggered.

Charley turned to George. "Has anyone come and asked you difficult questions lately?", he enquired. "George pondered for a few seconds, then pointed to a magnificent set of vases on a bureau on the same wall as the exit door. "Come to think of it, Yes. There was a chap who seemed very interested in that Sevres garniture over there, and I must have been talking to him for nearly five minutes, about twenty minutes ago." "What did he look like?", asked the boy, eagerly. "Nothing special", answered the guide. "Tallish, receding grey hair, and horn-rimmed glasses. I think he was wearing a lovat sports jacket and grey trousers." "I thought so", nodded Charley; "There's your distraction. Anyone could have done the lifting; all it needed was for someone to block the entrance doorway for a ten seconds, while the thing was picked up and put somewhere closer to the rope. But the carrying is not so easy." He pointed to a large Chinese export vase which stood on a table just inside the entrance to the room. "Is there anything in that?", he asked.

The Curator stepped across and reached inside the vase, bringing out a handful of sweet papers and chocolate wrappers. Somewhat guiltily he said:-" This only gets cleaned once a week". A gleam entered Charley's eye. "There you are; that's the lifting. They must have used those papers to stop any clinking. Now, how big was this marble, how much did it weigh and what did it look like?" George explained that the lost treasure was a putto, about ten inches high, weighing perhaps about four or five pounds. "Putty" interrupted Charley. "That explains it. I was wondering how anyone could lift a piece like that with one hand." The Curator began to look bemused at this apparent non sequitur. Charley's uncle steeped into the breach. "My nephew and I have been working on a theory which may upset the modern perception of a very important historical episode", he said. "Charley believes that Francis Drake was not playing bowls on Plymouth Hoe, but a form of marbles. The word 'marble' of course stems from the Old French 'marle', or clay, and 'boule', meaning ball or bowl. Thus we have an 'earthern ball' which must be hard and strong but sufficiently light in weight to be delivered over a considerable distance by one hand. With this interesting theory in mind, it did not occur to him that you were using the word 'marble' to describe a carved piece of crystalline limestone. Charley was looking for a spherical object of about six inches in diameter rather than a humanoid figure some ten inches in height."

Charley took up the running again. "Quite right, Unk, and I was thinking of our last experience of putty, which is of course quite light, being just powder stuck together with linseed oil. I think that all came out in The Case of the Pane in the Glass. But let's get on with the carrying. A long thin something is much easier to walk off with than a heavy ball." He turned to George again. " Have you had any wheelchairs round today?," he asked. "Not today", replied the guide. "Pity! They're always good for a hollow seat or something like that. What about fat men?" George looked suitably bewildered. "I think I do remember one short man who was very well built, with a large stomach and wide trousers," he said.

"That's it , then" said the boy detective triumphantly. "So your bit of marble was lifted by a gang of three including your tall man and a short fat man who put the piece down his trousers. Shouldn't be difficult to track down, though they must have got away before you pushed the alarm."

By this time there were several police officers busy making notes. At this stage they obviously couldn't think of a better explanation, so for the time being were going along with ideas from someone who had a successful track record.

The remaining public were released after having their names and addresses taken and the Hall returned to normal business, though certainly not too normal, for this was the last day of the opening season. Police investigations continued for several weeks thereafter, through the usual channels of informers, known criminals whose past modus operandi seemed to fit, and pleas to the antiques trade to be watchful. The latter was more in hope than anything else. The police had no great opinion of the morals of some influential members of that sector and suspected that more ownerless property than enough went through the secondary market. It was all to no avail. There was not a sniff of the Michelangelo Marble, from grasses and villains alike.

When the Hall had been closed for the night, and of course for the season, George collected from under his chair the briefcase which he brought to work each volunteer day, containing his sandwich box, a thermos flask and notes on the contents of the three rooms between which he alternated, and left for the winter. When he arrived home to his widower's flat, he took the flask to the sink, unscrewed the double cap - cup and cover- and dismantled the flask completely. It was wide-bodied and fairly tall, and the inside instead of being the single silvery glass vessel which one normally finds in such a piece of equipment, was in two parts, a carefully padded and dry receptacle underneath the top two inches, which consisted of a tiny silver jar full of black coffee. George withdrew the Michelangelo Marble and contemplated it lovingly. He was a real conoisseur of such beauty. That kid was a godsend, he thought to himself, but I think it would have worked anyway.

The next week saw him at London Airport ready to fly off with his light luggage on a short holiday to the USA, which he had publicised with enthusiasm among his friends and colleagues. He carried with him some sandwiches and his thermos flask, and a couple of books to read on the flight. There were of course as yet no such refinements as X-ray machines at airports, and he had nothing to declare to the customs officals who were really on the lookout for smuggled currency. His passport and visa were in order. As the plane lifted off, he took a last look at the country of his birth, and had no real regret to be leaving it.

Two weeks later, an American multi-billionaire collector stood in his private museum, gloating over the rare and stunningly beautiful figure of a putto, sculpted by genius-laden hands nearly five hundred years previously. He did not care that he was unable to proclaim ownership of this wonderful object. He knew he had got it, and a very few select friends might also get to see it - only of course those who had similar black collections and thus had a vested interest in keeping them totally secret.

Meanwhile, George sat comfortably in a first-class seat in a plane flying westward over the vast waters of the Pacific Ocean. He sipped his whisky as he watched the cotton-wool clouds float by, and heaved a long sigh of contentment. He was officially dead, having looked the wrong way while attempting to cross a busy street, and he now had a completely new and what appeared to be foolproof identity and was on his way to a superbly fitted bungalow on a Hawaiian beach, bought and registered in his new name. In his pocket was a bank statement showing a seven-figure dollar credit to his account "Isn't it wonderful what money can do," he thought, "and how lucky that people with money are prepared to spend any amount of it to gratify their childish whims." He raised his glass. "Here's to you, Mike, old boy", he whispered.

VILLAGE VENDETTAS

Imagine a small, sleepy village between the two great wars, close to the capital but not yet a part of it. There seems to no special reason for its existence on that particular spot, three miles equidistant from two market towns, except perhaps that it is on the main railway line to the coast. The village is beginning to grow, although the full impact of the rush for housing on a dormitory basis has not yet made itself felt and many of the streets are still unpaved. But it is still at heart a village, and as such harbours the same loyalties, dissensions, activities and information network which are to be found in communities set deep in the heart of a rural countryside.

The small railway station is beginning to assume an importance in the village, as the numbers of residents whose choice it is to commute each day to the metropolis slowly increase. There is method in this way of life, which provides a higher rate of income in return for extra time spent travelling, yet bestows also the benefits of living in a small, self-sustaining community in which there is scope for leisure, self-importance, social activities and charity. The village is close-knit, for practically everybody knows and is known to everyone else, so that the stationmaster will sometimes hold a morning city-bound train for a minute or two until Mr.Smith or Mr Brown has arrived. The frenzied urgency of metropolitan life has not yet penetrated this outpost of rustic peace.

The village consists of two parallel streets, running on either flank beside the railway line, with one lane crossing at a right angle which on one side leads on to the ancient coast road and on the other bends round to bisect a new concrete race track, dignified by the modern phrase "arterial road" and directed towards rapidly-growing industrial and residential developments on the great estuary. The centre possesses but one public house, but there is another a half-a-mile away on the hill road which winds up to commons, fields and woods in the widening gap between the two main roads.
The life of the village, however, does not depend on the provision of alcohol-lubricated centres of conversation. There are two churches and a tiny baptist chapel; a War Memorial Institute in which dances, classes, clubs, social organisations, scouts, guides, brownies and cubs may find a permanent home, all fitting together in a carefully and equitably planned timetable. The Institute, like the Church of England, is constructed largely of corrugated iron, though the church council is endeavouring to raise funds for a new, brick-built home.

For the benefit of the younger children of slightly-better-off families, two elderly spinster sisters run a survival from a more gracious age - a Dame School from which five-year olds are able to emerge ready-equipped with basic reading, writing and arithmetical skills, nurtured by the gentle care of the sisters and enforced with hot milk and chocolate fingers at mid-morning break. It is not clear whether this stolen march on the education front helps or hinders the staff of the low, red-brick infants' and junior school a few hundred yards away, but the school's record of scholarship examination passes and onward progression to higher education is among the best in that part of the county.

In addition to the everyday side of education, the arts are not forgotten, and piano lessons are given, in her own home on a magnificent black German upright piano, by a charming but ancient widow who in her day has performed before the crowned heads of Europe with a zither orchestra.

Apart from the many activities in the Memorial Institute, leisure is catered for by a small part-time County library and the beginnings of a recreation ground incorporating the village cricket and football fields and a playground for the children. Sadly, despite the efforts of the junior-school headmaster, a man of sound, old-fashioned ideas as to education and upbringing, and his small staff, and notwithstanding the facilities for both mechanically assisted and free, field-and-ditch play offered by the recreation ground, not all the children are satisfied. Already their very natural urge to progress to adulthood long before they are properly fitted to do so has engendered tragedies.

One small boy, old enough to know better but playing with his friends the dangerous game of "Chicken" has paid the dreadful, supreme penalty and brought grief, doubt and anxiety to the village. "Chicken", for those of modern generations which have been precluded from such activities by the very pace of life and the growth of urban concrete and traffic, is a stupid and deadly game which involves children in an unnecessary and false challenge which nonetheless if not accepted strikes deeply at their self esteem and thus becomes nigh irresistible. The winner is simply the last of a group to dart successfully across a road in the face of oncoming traffic. It is perhaps fortunate that at the time of this sad event there was not very much traffic, and that it did not move at the relentless and malignant speeds which in years to come would make English roads a lottery of life and death. But one small boy slipped on gravel and was caught a glancing blow by the oncoming bus which he had selected as an adversary. The driver, slowly as he was moving, had no chance to avoid the child, and the stunned passengers dismounted to gather in shock around a little, crumpled body whose life and promise had departed in a small pool of blood.

After living in a state of horror for some weeks, strong admonitions being delivered daily in homes and in the school, the village recovers its equilibrium. The effects on future juvenile behaviour of either the scoldings or the pathetic example cannot be assessed, but it is to be hoped that some good will emerge from the tragedy. Sadly it is acknowledged that this will be of no comfort to the boy's family. The fact that the accident took place close to the school itself is the cause of much self-reproach among the teaching staff, but naughty children kept after school have to be attended to, the next day's lessons must be prepared, and there are no lollipop ladies. For a long while afterwards, parents meeting their children from school redouble their watchfulness and shout loudly at examples of foolishness and derring-do, but their hands are full enough without accepting on a permanent basis responsibilty for others.

There is even a hint of unwonted tolerance of some of the less dangerous childish activities. Housewives answering a knock or a ring at their front door, only to catch a glimpse of a small shoe and a wrinkled, half-mast sock disappearing round the corner of the hedge have been known, instead of shouting (or worse - mouthing) imprecations, to limit their reactions to a grumbled "Well - better Knock-down-Ginger than Chicken, I suppose." Crimes against property, though, have not reduced in seriousness and the scrumping of apples continues to be regarded as a heinous offence. Funnily enough, the disappearance of pears in similar fashion has never seemed to matter so much. Perhaps this is because pears are picked quickly when ripe, so that any taken by scrumping are likely to be hard and green, and calculated to carry with them their own punishment in the shape of grievous youthful bellyache.

The life-blood of the village, literally and socially, is exactly what it always is in small, compact communities - the Shop. Or rather, in this case, the shops, for the population is too large to be satisfied with just one all-embracing village store. Indeed, along the streets either side of the railway there has grown up what is almost a foretaste of the later-day small shopping centre. There are two newsagents and confectioners, one either side of the tracks; no less than two grocers, three butchers, a baker, a dairy, a hardware store, a cobbler, a pharmacy, two greengrocers, a post-office, a bicycle shop, a doctor and a dentist, a hairdresser and (last but by no means least) an off-licence. The latter is by now a necessity. Few houses are without sherry or port, mainly for Christmas but sometimes for special occasions or visitors. Spirits are not to be found in many sideboards, but the fashion is fast growing for tonic wines as a health aid - Sanatogen and Wincarnis, to mention but two. However, rustic frugality has not been superseded by the new city-led affluence, and the relative cost of less advertised substitutes has not escaped the notice of the tonic-seekers.

The off-licence has a huge business in Australian burgundy, presented in the "bocksbeutel" in which Franconian wine has always been found. And much of its trade, too, comes from the children's unceasing consumption of such drinks as lemonade, ginger beer, ice-cream soda, dandelion and burdock and sarsparilla.

The largest establishment of all is the head office of a family firm of millers, seedsmen and corn merchants, whose shop at the entrance to a cobbled yard surrounded by barns, stables and other outbuildings sells a great variety of garden tools and requisites, as well as flour and grains, all amid an unmistakeable smell of agriculture. The firm's great horses and drays are a common sight around the village, usually followed by children bearing buckets and shovels in order to earn a few coppers in exchange for fertiliser for their fathers' roses.

Thus we have a birdseye view of this community, but it would be completely wrong to make the assumption that within it, in houses, cottages, shops or in the Institute or the waiting rooms of the station, the doctor and the dentist, placidity and harmony reigns serenely and supremely. For that is certainly not the case. The community is a group of people, and people can be Trouble with a capital "T", especially when they congregate in groups.

The following events took place in the village over a period of years, but time and history merge so that many happenings blur together and often become indistinguishable. First, however, it should be understood that under the surface of many an apparently peaceful village community there bubble and boil seething spots of dissatisfaction, envy, real or perceived injustice, misunderstanding and sometimes even outright hatred. In England the Italian vendetta in its pure sense of a family blood-feud no longer exists, but without the blood it is far from uncommon. The village had an average share of internecine disputes, and there were brothers who had not spoken to each other for forty years, and women who crossed to the other side of the street when they saw their sister approaching. Inter-family quarrels, however were a constant source of gossip and entertainment.

Some of these quarrels sprang from the days when parties of the young village set would pile into their Austin Sevens and drive off to the coast for weekends which looked for sunshine but would not be ruined if the alternative were to be huddling together in secluded places, sheltering from the rain. Many romances were started, many were ended, and not a few partners were changed so that previously inseparable groups were left in tatters and social and diplomatic relations were broken off. But, in fairness, many happy and fruitful marriages resulted, even if the crop ripened a bit early.

In other instances, flimsy excuses and insignificant events caused friendships, sometimes of long-standing, to break down. The Burtons ceased to have dinner with the Jacksons on alternate Fridays in their respective houses after Mr. Jackson was thought to have passed harsh comments on Mrs Burton's steak-and-kidney pudding. Mrs Biggs stopped speaking to her close friend Mrs Gooch as a result of a chance remark as to the cleanliness of curtains, and Mr Parsons accused his childhood mate Mr Dale of cheating at Nap.
One particularly blatant example was the severance of contact between next-door neighbours who had for years on a Saturday evening sat together, family with family, in blissful enjoyment around a table containing a vast bowl full of winkles and several packets of pins. So close had the Baileys and the Bradleys become that a communicating gateway had been cut into the fence between the two back gardens, so that the children could play together without going into the street and the wives could pop into each other's kitchen for a nice cup of tea. Alas, when Mrs Bradley accused Mrs Bailey of throwing a pail of washing-up water over her cat Smokey, the husbands were ordered to nail up the fence again as a symbolic gesture signifying the end of a beautiful friendship.

And so it went on, but so too did the life of the village, its surface undisturbed except in the way that ripples on a pond may indicate some piscine drama taking place beneath.

A questing outsider (assuming, that is, that he was permitted to find out anything) might have discovered that the commerce of the village, though mainly amicable, was spotted with small but bitter arguments between traders. A change of allegiance on the part of an unsuspecting housewife, for no reason other than perhaps of convenience, might cause accusations of customer-poaching. Price-cutting was seriously frowned upon as unfair competition. Encroachments or overlaps among traditional merchandise met with complaint - the butchers would take up arms against a grocer who attempted to sell meat, as would the confectioners against the off-licence or any other establishment which attempted to muscle in on the trade for liquorice boot-laces or sherbert dabs. And there was continual bad blood between Mary Clark at the dairy and George Chapman who kept a small herd of cows just outside the village and sold milk from the cart which he and his horse paraded through the village each morning, including Sunday. George scorned the trouble and expense of bottles or cartons. What had been the norm for a hundred years of milk-selling was good enough for him, and he solemnly poured milk straight from churns into the jugs brought out by his customers, using a narrow can-shaped, vertically-handled ladle. Not even the subtitle of Mary's shop, or its hygenic, sparkling-white appearance could attract the custom of the entire village. But both George and The Pure Milk Supply Dairy continued in business.

In many of these small disputes, acrimony often continued when its cause had long been forgotten, and lasted sometimes even unto the next generation. It was fortunate that in the case of the newsagents, the grocers. the greengrocers and to a certain extent the butchers, there were shops on each side of the railway, for the village people tended for shopping purposes to keep to their own side of the tracks. There was therefore no youthful competition between the newsboys who rose early to deliver their quota of papers before going to school.

It was a telling comment upon the leisure life of the community that the atmosphere of dispute should exist also in some of the clubs and societies in the village. Such meritorious organisations as the guides, brownies, scouts and cubs bred nothing worse than healthy rivalry, mostly internal. The Scouting movement was at its best in this village atmosphere, the urban groups often operating in slightly different ways to combat their different environment. Fields and woods there were in plenty for the practice of outdoor skills, and parents could watch with pride their offspring marching in church parades, perhaps even carrying a flag or blowing a bugle. There were willing volunteers to oversee the troops and packs, and more than one young man or woman graduated through the ranks to become supervisory assistants, later moving on in life to greater things within a broader community.

Some of the rivalries in the groups which centred on the Institute were both natural and good-natured, though this was not always the case. An amateur theatrical group was among the early societies, putting on regular performances of the popular plays of the time. Such groups are of course notorious for arguments over the suitability of players chosen for particular parts, and it was not unknown for dark accusations to be made as to the existence of clandestine bribes or even casting couches There were dancing classes for children, a sewing club, the ubiquitous Women's Institute, a poetry-reading society, and regular Saturday-night dances. There were few evenings, and not that many afternoons, when the Institute was not in use.

Outdoor sports were well-supported. There was no dispute between the cricket club and the football club because, although the seasons overlapped, each had its own ground. In any case, many of the cricketers were also footballers, playing regularly in either friendly games against neighbouring clubs or more competitively as part of a league. In winter one might watch a right-back who during the week was a painter and decorator and in the summer hurled down his fast bowling on the cowering batsmen of opposing cricket teams. Equally a commuter with a fine eye for a ball and absolutely no training could be seen in summer striking several fours and sixes before being caught somewhere in close proximity to the boundary; his wicket was rarely broken. Later in the year, tall and commanding, there he would be as centre-half holding his team's defence together.

In the summertime there was some competition between cricket and tennis, though tennis was played regularly on Sunday afternoons, whereas this was not always so with cricket. Surprisingly, the tennis club became the centre of a famous dispute which lasted for several seasons and even involved the local churches.

The small Baptist chapel kept itself very much to itself and upset no-one with the possible exception of men in the adjacent houses whose Sunday slumbers might have been disturbed by the over-fervent singing of Baptist hymns. The Methodist church was across the tracks at the bottom of an estate of new and relatively up-market houses, and was screened from the street by a straggling row of trees which gave the boys of the village much enjoyment by way of swinging in the fashion of Tarzan of the Apes from one end of the row and back again, all without touching the ground. At the time of the dispute, the Church of England was being re-sited , also from across the tracks, to a plot near the school and not far from the tennis club.

When lines were drawn for the forthcoming battle, the Methodists tended to side with the club, unsurprisingly since the thriving Youth Club at their church was accorded the use of the tennis courts on one evening each week during the season. The Church of England, however, was led by a vicar of strong and traditional beliefs who deplored publicly the fact that Sunday tended to be the busiest day at the tennis club.

The club itself was situated in the middle of a rectangle formed by streets mostly lined with houses, and access was through an unmade back entry serving some of those properties. Fortunately, the space was large enough not to create too many problems of proximity to impinge on either the privacy or the hearing of the residents. The ground was, in fact, owned by one of the residents who'for many years was himself a playing member. There were three grass courts, maintained on a rota system by the members. The club pavilion was an old wooden building which provided rudimentary changing facilities, a small kitchen with a serving hatch, an open-sided space for the protection of spectators from sun or rain, and a room which held a table-tennis table much used by senior and junior members alike. What, you might think, was there to dispute about such an apparently satisfactory set-up?

Well, the problem was one of usage. A local speculative builder wished to buy the land together with an unused field next door, and erect thereon as many houses as possible. The owner was not in favour of these plans, valuing his privacy and his loyalty to the club more highly than a cash windfall, especially as he knew that beside the profit to be made by the builder his would pale into insignificance. So the matter was stalemated, but the club members lost no opportunity to taunt the builder and his supporters whenever the chance arose. It is to the credit of the other party that no attempt was made to dig up the tennis courts on a dark night. Predictably the intervention of the vicar on grounds of Lord's Day Observance fell on stony ground.

The whole affair seems now to have been too insignificant to warrant more than a day or so's argument. But in fact it went on for several years, flaring up occasionally when brought into unrelated disputes as a back up at times when relevant material either ran out or did not exist at all. There was in fact no physical violence, and brother was not set against sister, nor mother against son. The situation was there, and would continue to be there for as long as the owner's allegiance to the tennis club held firm, or until he died, and it was later found that he had left the land to the club anyway. Participants were resigned to the fact that the dispute would continue to simmer long after their playing days were over, but it did not upset their enjoyment of their tennis.

The end came suddenly and unexpectedly when the second war broke out. A nation in no way prepared for war tried hard to make up for lost time, and the Spanish Civil War had told them that they had to think about the civilian population as well as the armed forces. Large communal, partly submerged air raid shelters were hurriedly built, and what better site than one close to the greatest number of houses. So part of the spare space around the club pavilion was dug up and a shelter constructed. The final blow fell when submarine attacks began to threaten the food supply, and the message "Dig For Victory" was heard throughout the land. The club and its landowning benefactor accepted defeat for themselves in the greater cause of national victory, and the tennis courts were turned into allotments and the pavilion into a toolshed.

To this day no member of the Church of England congregation has volunteered any information as to whether or not specific thanks were offically offered up during the next Harvest Festival service. The speculative builder went broke, despite the fact that houses were tumbling and creating vacant space all around him. The Methodist Youth Club bought two extra table-tennis tables, secondhand, and a wag member of the defunct tennis-club summarised the entire situation one evening in the local pub. "It's not a case of "Sic transit gloria mundi", he said, but "Sic transit thirtyall Sunday".

BOOKSHOP

Through the door of the bow-fronted shop at the end of a narrow passage off the High Street could be seen nothing but shelves of books, all, however, carefully arranged in logical sequence so that Anthony Turner, the proprietor could put his hand on almost any item, however obscure, at a moment's notice. Having been a Professor of Literature at Oxford, he had called his shop "Town and Gown", partly as a tribute to the old ways of the University and the vacillating relationships between the under-graduates and the townspeople, and partly because his first taste of University atmosphere had come from a book which had left him incurably romantic about it. Mr.Verdant Green had a lot to answer for.

After thirty years of an academic career, Anthony had decided to retire while he was still young enough to dabble in a field which reflected his life-long interest in the printed word. The secondhand book shop had just come on the market on the death of its previous owner who, well into his seventies, had tended to let things slide. The premises were dingy, the stock was more suited to a period fifty years into the past, the clientele was spasmodic - a handful of old guard professors, a sprinkling of undergraduates trying to pick brains which, being two generations old, might not be recognised in modern translation, - and the usual complement of collectors looking for bargains. And probably finding them, too, thought Anthony on his first look at the shop. He was comfortably off and could afford if necessary to indulge a whim or two, so he completed the purchase, lock and stock but without the barrel, and set about the enormous task of making order out of at least twenty years of chaos.

Having often thought idly of the possibility of his retirement taking this particular form, he had quite a few pre-conceived ideas for attracting people to the shop and persuading them to buy. He spent money along these lines on the premises themselves, before worrying too much about the stock. That, he decided, he would buy selectively himself, and he set aside two days, out of the six-day week, on which the shop would not open, so that he could travel afield buying to a carefully balanced list of wants. Indeed, these days on the move he soon found the most fascinating part of the whole project. He had meanwhile opened, relying temporarily on the old man's stock and utilising the time between customers in sorting and cataloguing what was already there, getting rid of the books he didn't want and evolving a plan for the new geography which was going to be necessary in order to fulfil his ambition to offer an arrangement which should be equally logical to the customers and efficient for himself. On his field trips he took care to note how other shops went about all this, and soon found obvious system faults which he was thus able to avoid.

In the reception area immediately inside the front door of the shop he sited his own command post. There he intended to ask incoming browsers to leave in his care any bags which they had with them, explaining in a prominent notice the necessity for this rule, and apologising for any inconvenience, etc. To forestall potential arguments he decided to install a small numbered rack and issue tokens which could be redeemed at the cash-desk nearby. That way there should be no chance of bags bring removed by persons other than their rightful owners.
The shop was to be devoted exclusively to literature, mainly English and mainly twentieth century, in all its aspects from poetry to science fiction and fantasy. The stock in the front area was to consist of first or elaborately-bound editions and other rare volumes; he had found this common practice in many shops.
Behind, towards the rear of the premises, the shop became two rooms wide, with a central dividing passageway going back three rooms deep, so that in addition to the door area there were six good-sized rooms. Some of these already possessed a full complement of shelving, serviceable if not exactly handsome.
Anthony decided to extend this arrangement to fill each room from floor to ceiling, and provided libary steps, one set for each two rooms. Meanwhile much of the stock was piled on the floors, awaiting sorting into the major categories which he had identified as appropriate to his evolving master-plan.

This plan was simple and basic. The emphasis everywhere was to be on the authors themselves, so three of the rooms were allocated for an alphabetical display under authors' names. Never, unless in exceptional circumstances, were more than two authors to occupy the same section of shelving. There was a very good reason for this. It was Anthony Turner's intention to group under an author's name not merely his works but also relevant and specific biographical and critical books; in due course he also hoped to add a cross-index to other volumes which contained multi-person references, and were to be found in the fourth room, arranged in order of critical author under a selection of sub-headings.

Beyond these four rooms the resemblance to other bookshops ceased. In room five there were several writing-tables, on which bona-fide researchers were permitted to work, using the stock of the shop as a library. The shelves in this room were devoted to catalogues, indexes, and cross-references, with some past published dissertations thrown in for good measure; Anthony hoped that in due course these might be increased in number by the generosity of grateful students who had taken advantage of the facility offered. He also acquired part-runs of some of the magazines which dominated the early part of the twentieth century, both critical and popular, for many a famous author had got his start by means of serialisation in such publications as "Strand", "Windsor", "Pall Mall", and "Hearth and Home". In the other, more serious section could be found "Adelphi", "New Age" and particularly "The Bookman". There was no charge for this service, but anyone wishing to take advantage of it had to show references from academic sources.

Within only a few months of opening, the demand had become so great that a booking system had to be started. The University authorities, at first somewhat sceptical, soon came to look on the venture with approval, realising that it might well increase the standard of dissertations submitted for literature degrees.

But it was in room six that Anthony had played his master-stroke. Here, the walls were lined mainly with his science fiction and fantasy stock, but in the centre of the room were clustered comfortable chairs into which customers were invited to sink and try out a book before buying. It was of course necessary to restrict the length of any one occupation, so after careful thought Anthony had decided on a system similar to that found in many city centre car parks:- "Maximum stay thirty minutes; no return within one hour". In order for this to run smoothly, expense had not been spared and a timed ticket system , with periodic visual checks has been instituted. Like the research room, the reading room was free and always full.

There were no upper floors to the shop. Behind a discreetly locked door in the front section was a staircase leading to Anthony's lavishly-furnished living accommodation. This was indeed a private holy-of-holies to which few people penetrated, not even the assistants whom at an early stage he had found it necessary to employ. Each one was hand-picked, all proved worthy of his trust and few ever left, some staying on for many years. Anthony Turner was a private man, with few friends; those who came into that category were all bookmen who formed with him a permanent natural bond based on their consuming interest. His own tastes were wide. It was perhaps as a result of the romantic streak which had caused Mr. Verdant Green to stick in his fancy that he quickly came to appreciate the classic side of fantasy fiction. For him it was a logical development of the novel, in which human characteristics and reactions were intermixed with supernatural, alien, inhuman - call it what you will - attributes, events and settings. There was of course a sidestream devoted to the exploration of the vexed question of afterlife and communication, physically or mentally, between the two worlds of the living and the dead. It was this interest which had led him to put his fantasy and science fiction stock in the reading room.

The years passed and the bookshop prospered. Once he had passed the official age of retirement, Anthony began to delegate a lot of the buying trips, though he still went off occasionally himself, in a much more leisurely fashion than at the beginning of the venture. Among his fantasy reading he been particularly attracted by an American book, to which he had been directed by a chance look at a film on television. The film was "Field of Dreams", based on the book "Shoeless Joe", by W.P.Kinsella, who had won a prestigious American literary award. Its theme was broadly speaking that of return from death to complete business unfinished in life. No matter how many times he watched the film, Anthony experienced the prickling of his scalp and the tingling of every nerve-end in his body which so often accompanies the indication of some supernormal atmosphere. He never failed to shiver at the voice from the Beyond whispering "If you build it, he will come".

So it was that as he got older, Anthony took to coming downstairs after his evening meal and sitting alone in the reading-room with several books by one or two authors, in the hope that he might receive a visitation from their shades. The feeling of physical anticipation came on a few occasions, without any further result. It may have been this which led him secretly to instal a sound-recording system with an automatic start-on-sound mechanism. He did not tell his friends. Dedicated as they were, he did not expect them to have the obsessional faith which he himself had developed.

It therefore came as a surprise to his staff to find him dead one morning, sprawled peacefully in his chair in the reading-room, with an opened book on the floor in front of him and a slight smile on his face. It came as an even greater surprise to his literary executors to discover the complicated recording system. They took out the cassette, and found that it had been in use. The three of them sat down to listen to what was on it, in the hope that there might be some sort of last-minute instructions to them.

The recording started with a click, followed by the scraping of a chair being pushed back and the sound of voices apparently going through a formal introduction process. Then, more chairs were moved as the owners of the voices sat down. "I ssssee you have been rrreading G-G-Gilchrist", said the first voice, high-pitched and with the slightest hint of a rasp behind the stutter. "Wwwhat do you think of him?". Anthony Turner's voice followed:- "Definitely

under-rated. He should never have been ignored as he was after his death." The other voice went on:- "There you are, Hughie, I've always ttold you how much I rregretted not pushing his sstuff more;" As the voice grew more animated, the stutter receded:-" Mind you, Phillpotts did his best with that ccollection of short stories and his preface was excellent." A third voice took up the conversation, a mildly resonant baritone, with upper-middle class enunciation and an apricottish rather than a plummy quality:- " Don't forget me, Arnold. Remember what I said about him in "The Apple Trees". "True", replied the first voice. "But you said more about his person than you did about his books. Don't deceive yourself, Hughie. You know you thought the world of him. And you certainly succeeded in anticipating by years the current-day significance of the word when you called him 'a large gay figure' ".
The voice tittered, rather coarsely, before going on:- " Not that I care in the slightest about that; Robert Murray Gilchrist was a better writer of short stories than anyone else of his generation, including thee and me, and I am very glad to see that he has not, after all, been totally forgotten. I know myself how aggravating that can be." "Not you, Arnold", chuckled the other; "No-one could ever forget you for long!" The voice changed in tone:- "Look here, I think our friend is on his way; perhaps we should go with him." There came a long, breathy sigh, not of pain but of peace, followed by the noise of a book falling to the floor, and then silence, before the machine clicked off. The executors picked up the three books from the floor beside the chair:- "The Old Wives' Tale", "Rogue Herries", and "A Peakland Faggot". "It's not possible", gasped one of them; "Bennett, Walpole and Gilchrist".

The details of those few minutes were never revealed. The fate of the audio-cassette is unknown except to me and my fellow executors. And none of us can be sure exactly what we heard. Was it a last, light-hearted charade on the part of our dying friend, who did have a small talent for vocal impersonation? Or was it - well, - is there life after death and can the veil between the two be rent in certain circumstances? These are questions which I cannot answer, but if you go today to the Town and Gown bookshop, still famous and flourishing, you can see the chair in which Anthony Turner died, and on the shelves behind, out of their usual places in the "Authors" section, three books -by Arnold Bennett, Hugh Walpole and Robert Murray Gilchrist. The rest, as they say, is silence.

LITTLE MISS MADAME

Neither my son nor my daughter wanted a family. Both opted for a career and unencumbered leisure time to go with it. As a consequence, my wife and I went through middle age in the knowledge that we were totally unlikely to have grandchildren; she would occasionally look wistfully at the many offspring of our friends' children and there were a few moments of reflection when I was sorry that my direct line would become extinct when my own children died. I was by then the patriarch of a diminishing family.

By the time I was close to the age generally recognised as the biblical sell-by date, I had established a busy, probably overloaded retirement life style and it therefore came as a bombshell when my daughter suddenly announced at the age of forty that she intended to have a child. I was not amused, though my wife was delighted. I could foresee major problems affecting some of my many activities and involvements, for I knew that my conscience would never allow me to treat this unexpected addition to the family in any other way than one which accorded with my highest conception of the duties of a grandparent.

The birth duly took place. My wife was present at the messy, unexpected Caesarean and held the baby girl even before its mother was able to do so. Time passed. From the helpless bundle which came home from the hospital there grew a stocky, determined and intelligent infant with brilliant red hair, just like her mother's had once been. We did not see an awful lot of Lizzie - for that was the name by which she became generally known, the original 'Elizabeth' having succumbed to an abbreviation after good intentions to the contrary had gone with many of their fellows to pave the road to Hell.
But when she was very young she at least became accustomed to our presence and did not object to being held, bathed or changed by her doting grandmother. Personally I limited my involvement to the holding part. Things did not go completely without complications, as it was found that Lizzie's hips were dislocated and she had to spend several months in the discomfort of a splint which seemed, however, to sort the problem out by the time she came to crawl and then walk, both at a fairly early age. Talking too came early and at two years old Lizzie could hold an intelligent conversation.

Unfortunately at the same time she fell victim to the "Terrible Twos" syndrome and became sometimes fractious, demanding and totally exasperating. This, as even I must admit, was contrary to her normal temperament. Overall she was an intelligent, responsive, individual little person, and could be as good as gold when it suited her. I suppose in a way she was too advanced for her own good. Although she would happily play for hours on her own, she liked nothing better than to have attendant adults sprawled on the floor with her, holding conversations and playing out small dramas through the "little people" who inhabited her dolls' house and other toys. "Play with Lizzie", she would demand, and it was difficult to refuse.

Frequently there would appear in her conversation words of which the source defied identification - had she picked them up at home, at the baby-minder's or from the TV, on which her favourite was for some time the Tellytubbies. On one occasion her mother interrupted her play on her toy kitchen, asking her to do something, and was met with the polite but forceful answer :- "Actually, Mummy, I am extremely busy at the moment". There is no real answer to that, coming from a two-and-a-half-year old!

We exchanged visits. Lizzie came to our house, and we went to hers. Not particularly frequently, but sufficiently for her to accept us as part of her life and to feel comfortable with us. She would even on occasion talk to us briefly on the telephone. She called us Granny and Grand-dad, which still came out slightly garbled, as Ganny and Gan-Gan. She was vulnerable and unsettled in some respects, but almost without fear. On one visit to us she had wanted to feed the ducks, and as we had no bread was quite prepared to sacrifice one of her special small packets of savoury nibbly bits, which she called 'tigs'. She stood beside the lake, on which the ducks had been joined by a lone swan. Knowing the strength and reputed irascibility of swans we took extra care. She was not bothered in the slightest, but continued to throw her tigs into the water in the general direction of the birds. Unfortunately she forgot to let go of one, and the swan in reaching for it nipped her finger with its beak. She howled for a few seconds, but was satisfied that she was not permanently disabled and with our explanation that it was not really Mr Swan's fault, as he had thought that she was giving the tig to him. Next day we went again to the park. "Do you want to go and see if Mr.Swan is there again today?" I asked. She nodded. "Yes" she said; "Lizzie not go ----" and she threw out her arm in a hurling motion.

Two special types of play were expected of us. For one we were summoned by loud shouts of "Gan-GAN" to go upstairs to her bedroom/nursery and dance solemnly, with appropriate actions, to some of her favourite tapes, so we soon got to know all about the Wombles, Rosie and Jim and their like. Her reaction to music had been strong since she was still a tiny baby and would happily go to sleep to the sound of the Benny Goodman Quartet. From an early age, too, she always loved to be carried round the room and hold conversations with or receive explanations of the pictures and photographs on the walls. Long after she was too heavy for my wife to lift up, she would come to me, stretch out her arms and command "UP", and point gravely to the pictures which she wished to visit.

The other favourite was to be told stories - not from books, though she enjoyed those too, but from personal and private history. "Tell Lizzie a story 'bout Ganny fall off her bike", she would say, or ask for the involved but truthful tale of how when I was young the chimney sweep would come to sweep the chimney. Having attracted our attention, she would wait for us to sit down and then climb up beside us and snuggle comfortably into one arm while we either read or narrated the things she wanted to hear. Most of all she loved being told how her grandmother held her while her mother was still being stitched up, and this invariably resulted in a request to inspect the scar. It also led to an interest in doctors. "Doctor come and fix Lizzie"", she would say, having engineered a pretend accident to herself or perhaps to one of her little people, and we would have to bring forth a pretend doctor walking on two fingers and asking loudly " Who needs fixing now", before producing a pretend screwdriver and dabbing at the appropriate place saying "Fix, Fix,Fixed" to the accompaniment of contented and delighted little giggles.

This medical interest was a godsend when my daughter had to go into hospital for a couple of days for a minor female operation. In the thirty-odd months since her birth, Lizzie had never been separated overnight from her mother. She had breast-fed much longer than average, and showed no signs of stopping - though by then it was not for food but for comfort - until she suddenly decided that she was a big girl, not a baby, and gave it up after a very short tail-off period. For this reason, and probably because she was not all that close to her father, who by that time had left, the bond between mother and daughter was of great strength, and of extreme importance to them both. Lizzie was prepared for some days to accept that Mummy was going into hospital to have her bottom fixed because it was hurting, and that Granny and Grand-dad would be looking after her. She appeared not to be perturbed.

We duly arrived the day before the hospital bed was available. Next morning we set off on the premise that Lizzie was going to see Mummy safely tucked up in bed in the hospital and would then come home with Granny and Grand-dad.

Halfway there, in heavy rain we suddenly had to stop the car (fortunately under a bridge) because Lizzie threw up violently over her clothing and the car-seat. Hastily we disembarked, cleaned up the mess and changed her clothes and were able to continue on our way; she was not ill, I think, but tired and perhaps a bit stressed, and I had a sneaking suspicion that perhaps I shouldn't have given her that small drink of "ginger-pop" at breakfast time.

We arrived at the hospital with time to spare; indeed the bed wasn't even ready, but after a short wait in a small and somewhat dismal room from which we could at least see the streets below, Mummy was able to get into bed, be tucked in and cuddled - twice as it happened, as we had one false start to the leaving process. The rest of the day was not too bad. By dint of constant play and a long bath-time incorporating many unauthorised pleasures for Lizzie, we got her to bed and the night passed without too many problems.

Next morning we phoned and arranged to go in for a visit in mid-afternoon, so in the morning we explained the programme to Lizzie, put her in her push-chair and set off for the park. She was fine. Her favourite play was to swing on and on and on, propelled constantly by an attendant adult because she had not yet learn to swing herself with her legs. The slide was not very slippery due to a bit of rain, but she enjoyed walking (assisted, of course) on equipment reminiscent of an Army assault course and obviously intended for older children. She also acted most graciously, though not uncharacteristically, in giving a small boy some of her chocolate buttons. Then we put on her wellington boots and proceeded to the small stream which bisected the park. There, she paddled around, throwing countless stones at random into the water and thoroughly enjoying herself. Having persuaded her to leave the small beach, we continued round the park, playing Poohsticks at each bridge over the stream. Lizzie was absolutely no trouble.

On the return trip through many streets including a main road, my wife paid for this trouble-free morning. She was commanded to sing. What should she sing? "Off to see a wizard" came the immediate reply, so for some way we progressed to the accompaniment of part of the soundtrack of "The Wizard of Oz". When this palled, I exercised a modicum of diabolical adult cunning and had my wife singing to the tune of "Polly put the kettle on", over and over with the constant interjection of " Again! Again!", the magic words:- "Mummy's had her bottom fixed, and she'll soon be home!" I am pleased to record that I received many sympathetic looks from passers-by.

In the afternoon we set off again with the pushchair and travelled by tube into central London. We found our daughter repaired but in some pain, and a joyful reunion took place. We stayed for a couple of hours, with Lizzie alternating between the bed and a parade up and down the ward, staring at and sometimes conversing with nurses, patients and other visitors. She was not entirely at ease, I felt, in this alien atmosphere. Sure enough, soon after five she suddenly announced "Go back to Lizzie's house now," and saying farewell to her mother, with the promise that tomorrow it would all be over, we left. Again we had a false start, rather more serious than the previous one, but eventually we were propelling the pushchair, complete with a somewhat tearful Lizzie, down Tottenham Court Road in the business rush hour. Just short of Oxford Street a loud wail of "I want my Mummy" erupted from the chair. I bribed the child into temporary silence by means of a handful of chocolate buttons and we hastened down Charing Cross Road , looking fearfully behind us in the half-expectation of pursuit by wrathful commuters and/or police demanding "What are you doing with that child?"

At Cambridge Circus the buttons ran out. This time I employed a desperate stratagem. We knew that one of Lizzie's favourite outings was to a Macdonald's fast food emporium, so I looked her in the eye and promised her a nosh-up in the first such establishment we could find. "But YOU must look out for a Donno's", I said; that was what she called it; " and afterwards we'll take you to see the boats on the big river." Our luck was in. Just off St Martin's Lane we saw the tell-tale red sign and made for it much like medieval felons racing for ecclesiatical sanctuary with a posse of screaming peasants behind them. Sitting Lizzie on the counter, we asked her what she wanted, knowing full well that she would say "Nuggets". So we ordered a standard child's meal consisting of a few chicken nuggets, some chips, a small carton of tomato sauce, a cup of strawberry milkshake and a plastic toy. For ourselves, we couldn't face it. Fortunately there was an empty table and we sat for fifteen minutes while Lizzie entertained the other customers, particularly an obvious European tourist at the next table. In fairness, she offered us the odd chip, between munching her chicken nuggets and dipping her chips into the sauce, occasionally murmuring contentedly "Num Num; dip-dip chips; Nummy Scrummy". When we told her mother later on, she was horrified. "But she doesn't like tomato sauce," she said.

Supper over, we redeemed our promise and sauntered down Villiers Street to the embankment. There, with care, I stood Lizzie on the wide parapet of the river wall while we watched the boats go by , large and small, fast and slow, and tried to answer the tortuous but perversely logical questions which children ask when they are confronted with something different. Carried away by the euphoria of having got so far in comparative safety, I promised a trip in a big boat, fortunately at some future but currently indeterminable date. That promise has still to be kept, but it will be or there is likely to be big trouble.

By that time we reckoned that the trains would be less crowded, so we dived down through the tube station and managed to get on the first train which came in. We did not immediately get seats, but stood at the end of the compartment. A seat came up quickly and my wife sat down. "I want to sit on a big seat like Ganny" said Lizzie. ""So you shall", I replied, "as soon as there is an empty one next to Granny". Which there was, shortly, so I lifted the child out of the pushchair and placed her on the vacant seat. "You must hold on tight", said my wife, " because this train bumps about and you might fall off." She reinforced this instruction by putting an arm round the little girl.
Opposite was a young woman who, though pretending to be reading her book, could not take her eyes off this spectacle of a small girl sitting solemnly inspecting the other inhabitants of the carriage and talking the while in a patently adult fashion. Lizzie pointed to a tall man sitting nearby, his long legs planted firmly halfway across the floor. "That man isn't holding on ", she complained. Thinking quickly, my wife explained that the man had long legs which reached to the floor, while she (Lizzie) had only short legs which didn't The explanation was gracefully accepted. On the next seat to Lizzie sat another man, immersed in a magazine. Lizzie looked at him curiously. He crossed his legs. Lizzie crossed her legs. He uncrossed his legs. Lizzie uncrossed hers. The young woman opposite was having great difficulty in not bursting into laughter. And so the ride continued, uneventfully and peacefully. We emerged into the gathering dusk and walked home, stopping only to buy a couple of bits from the supermarket.

The evening went well. Lizzie was tired and had already had something to eat. After some play, some stories and the reiterated promise that Mummy would be home the next day, we bathed her and put her to bed. She slept fairly quickly.

At about three in the morning I leapt out of sleep at the sound of repeated cries of "I want my Mummy". I lifted the child from her bed, held her close, patted her and stroked her hair, walking up and down the room explaining that Mummy's bottom was now all fixed and that she would be home soon. The sobbing continued for a while, but gradually stopped. I returned the small, warm body to the bed, tucked her in carefully in the way in which she always insisted upon, kissed her and stood looking down at her. Her beautiful, liquid, soulful eyes met mine. "Gan-Gan", she said " I'm all right now. You can go." Obediently I withdrew from the Presence, walking backwards and bowing deeply, and returned to bed.

MANY A SLIP

The so-called Industrial Revolution began in the mid-18th century and lasted at most for 250 years. It was set off by improvements in technology and a self-feeding market demand; and it was ended by improvements in technology and the need to stimulate demand. The age of the ponderous mechanical dinosaurs was a tiny grain in the sands of time, like the ages of stone, and bronze and iron, in each of which lessons from the past were simply relearned, taken to the extended limits offered by new technology and expanded in the light of fresh knowledge acquired incidentally. No doubt from the time when man first picked up a fallen branch and defended himself with it, or attacked a potential food source, or possibly even beat his wife, there was a wood age before all the others, when the early men found it possible to shape wood to perform various previously undreamed-of functions. As each new fresh material became workable, so the lessons went on and grew in complexity.

Thus, evolution constantly fathered revolution, and revolution, in its turn, gave way to the inexorable expansion of the new frontiers of evolution. When work previously possible only with the aid of massive machinery could be done by invisible currents of electricity or by controlled combustion, the wheel of progress completed a full revolution and the computer age began. Man, having successively broken to his will the elements of water and earth and fire, now sought to harness the mysterious minute powers of air and space. From water wheels to steam engines and on to internal combustion and jet propulsion he had progressed, and now reached out for the micro-secrets of atoms and the incredible mathematical storage capacity of tiny fragments of silicon.

All this happened quickly, and customs, habits, relaxations, pleasures and many other facets of human behaviour also began to change. The restricted and confined life of the Middle Ages had long ago given way to the wider horizons offered by swifter travel and communications. Cottage industries which had been essential to a closed community developed to serve larger areas. The old barter system had been one of the first casualties of the smaller world, but now farmers and craftsmen were able to present their produce and artefacts to a wider circle of people and a wider source of payment in coin. It also became possible to concentrate particular types of manufacture in districts wherein the necessary raw materials and fuel were readily available. Coal-mining districts, steel towns, agglomerations of mills to process cotton or wool - all these sprang up swiftly.

Alongside them developed communities of craftsmen who, realising the potential benefits of one small area catering for all major buyers of gloves, or hats, or shoes, were quick to overcome their natural antipathy to close competition.

And in an area of North Staffordshire, whose abundant supplies of coarse red clay and seams of fossil fuel had since the fifteenth century attracted the makers of earthenware utensils for domestic, dairy or farm use, a community of workers in clay started to grow more rapidly.
These "potters" were by no means as honest as they might have been, for in the 1660s or thereabouts it became necessary to pass an Act of Parliament to control their deceitful collusion with their agricultural customers in producing butter-pots containing less than they ought, by means of false sides and bottoms. They congregated at that time in the small town of Burslem. From here, the birthplace of Josiah Wedgwood and Enoch Wood, two of the greatest potters who ever lived, the industry spread rapidly outward to take in five other towns and innumerable villages and hamlets, and eventually to become known all over the world as "The Potteries", of which Burslem was (and still is) the acknowledged Mother Town.

The towns, despite fierce opposition from within, federated in 1910 and in 1925 were dignified by His Majesty George V, on a royal visit, with the appellation of "City". It is not impossible that the King was anxious to shake the dust of the Potteries from his highly polished boots, for the usual local legends emphasising the uniqueness of the area and the uncompromising attitudes of its people have grown around this visit. It is said, for instance and obviously to typify the local unwillingness to waste anything whatsoever, that at the inevitable civic banquet the Mayor (shortly to become Lord Mayor) noticed that Her Majesty had carefully trimmed all the fat from her meat, and leaning towards her he removed the trimmings to his own plate with a remark indicating his disapproval of this extravagance.

There can be no doubt that the Queen did not understand a word of what he said to her, because the dialect of the Potteries is without question the most outlandish in England. The vowel sounds are consistently and for no apparent reason distorted. Words such as "down" become "dine", while "light" becomes "late" and "late" turns into "leet"; "piece" equals "pace" and vice versa; "talk" becomes "toke", and "can" changes simply into "con". It would be pointless to ask a potter "how to get to Stafford?", though he might possibly respond to a polite request as to "arfur goo Staffy". Consonants are elided mercilessly, prepositions are transposed without rhyme or reason and, worst of all, speech in this region which is relatively profligate with time is carried on with a rapidity which would not have disgraced the Machine Gun Corps. It may well take a foreigner as long as ten years of constant communication before he can actually begin to understand what the normally polite children say to him as he passes them at their play in the cobbled back alleys behind the small, now sadly often sub-standard, houses. Even the peevish, more moaning than sing-song, aesthetically grating accents of the Birmingham region can out of sheer frustration be preferable to the outlandish tongue spoken less than forty miles to the north.

But there are compensations. The Potteries folk are at heart kind and interested, and because of their repudiation of haste are always ready to pass the time of day in pleasant and polite conversation. Nonetheless they have also been accused of being so attentive to people that, for instance, a waitress might be so interested in talking to a diner that she unwittingly pours the soup into his lap. There is also little doubt that in the Potteries far too much is expected of buildings and machinery. For two centuries the ethos has been:- While it does its job - let it; if it breaks down - bodge it up, summed up in the terse phrase "If it ain't broke, dunna mend it!" There has been scant attention paid to such new-fangled ideas as a regular maintenance programme.

Nearly one hundred years on from the original federation, most of the small consituent areas of the so-called city still guard jealously their names and their individualities. At that earlier time, the Potteries were already past their hey-day, which really took place in the first half of the nineteenth century. But they had succeeded in cornering a large part of the world market for everyday domestic pottery and in introducing a great many types, styles, designs and processes which kept them in the forefront of the world industry until well after the 1939-45 war. In order to do this, the inhabitants of the Potteries resigned themselves to earning a living in conditions of considerable dirt, discomfort and danger, on work which was often monotonous and demanding, and yet which offered a visible end-product of a certain beauty and of an undoubted usefulness. Over the course of two centuries, the first fifty years being dominated by the vision, drive and commercial acumen of the great Josiah Wedgwood, the Potteries evolved a character of their own, unlike any other to be found even in comparable strongholds of manufacturing industry. There were some similarities For instance, the employment of women and children came early to the Potteries, as it did to the cotton towns of Lancashire, but in the Potteries the girls provided much of the artistic output, by way of hand-painting on the completed objects, and most (though not all) of the physcially arduous tasks were left to the men. Thus, the Potteries women became independent and self-confident, while the men, too, were jealous of their status as producers of useful beauty and, relieved to an extent of the complete burden of financial provision for their families, were able to gratify their thirsts after long days spent in an atmosphere of dust and heat.

That is not to say that they were all incorrigible drunkards, for they succumbed at an early stage to the stern discipline of Wesleyan Methodism; indeed it was in the Potteries that there first arose that austerest of all sects - the Primitive Methodists. Nonetheless it is a matter of record that in the town of Burslem around the end of the nineteenth century there were more than a hundred outlets for the sale of beer.

It was possibly the stirring music of the Chapels which led the area to become second to none in choral performance, which was later for a short time extended to an orchestra also. Amateur Operatic and Dramatic groups flourished in numbers well above average in relation to the size of the population, and one of the great moments in local musical history came when Elgar's work "King Olaf" was premiered in the Potteries.

In the years leading up to the second great conflict, after the depression was more or less over, the City of Stoke-on-Trent was perpetually covered by a pall of smoke of which the suspended particles drifted ever down on to the curtains and washing-lines of the womenfolk who (as that great chronicler of the area, Arnold Bennett, noted early in his career) fought day-by-day to achieve and retain the respectability guaranteed by the whiteness of their curtains and linen. No doubt (but I cannot prove it) this cleanliness, in accordance with the tenets of the preachers in the chapels of the time, was considered to be next to godliness and therefore an infallible indication of purity of soul.

The pall of smoke came from the grimy emanations of more than two thousand kilns which night and day were busy turning soft clay into hard pottery. In their endeavours to shut off the sky, these erections were ably assisted by the larger furnaces of several steelworks and the vast tips of colliery waste dotted around a landscape worthy of Dante. Of these kilns some explanation should perhaps be given at this point. Though varying in look and design, according to their intended usage, whether for basic firing or for the hardening of enamel decoration, these "Bottle-Ovens", so called for their outward appearance as a host of giant brick-built containers of liquids, all worked in more or less the same way. The outer shell - the "hovel"- was in fact no more than a method of protecting the inner oven, and on occasion was not needed when the oven itself was inside a normal building. It was the oven which was of prime importance. On a circular base which contained a number of firemouths appropriate to its diameter there stood a firm floor above the firespace, the whole surrounded by a brick construction narrowing at the top to a funnel-shaped chimney through which the smoke and burnt gases of combustion could rise through a similar opening in the hovel-top above to pollute the surrounding atmosphere. The pieces to be fired were stacked inside the oven through a narrow door which was then bricked up and the fires lit.

The wares were protected in part, by containers of coarse marl, from the deleterious effects of the smoke; these containers were called "saggars" - a word whose origins are ancient and uncertain. The usual explanation given is some sort of distortion of the term "safeguard", but this is not entirely supported by the fact that, in his great "Natural History of Staffordshire", published in 1686, Dr. Robert Plot refers to "shragers"; even allowing for the vagaries of seventeenth century spelling, this leaves a slight area of doubt. The craft of saggar-making is an ancient though simple one and has been immortalised through the radio programme "What's my Line?" in the episode which beat the panel by introducing a Saggar-maker's Bottom-knocker, who was a mere assistant to the master and contented himself with flattening a heap of fireclay marl into a sort of rough base for an incipient container, using a huge wooden mallet.

The main by-products of the fires, though not all their heat, was conducted up between the heaps of saggars through devices which were basically hollow cylindrical sections placed one on top of each other right up to the top of the kiln, and known as "pipe-bungs".
For between two and three days and nights the most important personage in the self-contained universe within each hovel was the kilnmaster. By his skills alone could a successful firing operation be completed. Watching regularly through small spy holes into the raging inferno within, and sometimes assisted by examination of withdrawable pyrometers and test-pieces, he would give his orders to the firemen to feed the furnace, or perhaps to suppress it by means of dampers at the top of the kiln. The pyrometer, a Josiah Wedgwood invention, is a cunning device for measuring the shrinkage of the clay (sometimes up to as much as 20 %) and equating this to the temperature required to bring it about.

At the end of the firing period, only the kilnmaster's constant vigilance had for three days stood between success and the disaster of ruination of the entire contents of the oven. Quite apart from his duty to his employers the kilnmaster had to answer also to his colleagues who, within the harsh terms of their employment were often paid only for pieces which, in circumstances totally beyond their own control, came "Good From Oven". Even to men whose forbears had battled and often won against the iniquities of the Truck Act, a failed oven was a major disaster.

When the fires began to subside and the heat to die down from the levels as high as 1400 degrees to which it might have risen, the danger was not over. The sooner the oven could be opened and cleared, the sooner a new load could be fired. And many a kilnman suffered from burnt hair or hands or throat or lungs through being sent in to unload an oven which was still far too hot for such an operation to commence in safety.

Perhaps the most telling point for posterity to remember about the bottle-oven, now of course destroyed by the Clean Air Act and replaced by the cleaner heat of gas or electricity, is the dreadful coincidence of the lethal nature of work on bottle-ovens and the local dialect, in which a kiln is always spoken of as a "Kill". The current-day inhabitants of the City are by no means anxious to retain too many reminders of their grim industrial heritage, and the two thousand bottle-ovens have been reduced to a mere forty or so; many of these are in a state of disrepair and decay and despite the efforts of historical and heritage societies their number may diminish yet further.

The processes of the industry are simple, though to the uninitiated they may not appear so. The basic material is clay, often produced by the decay of granite or other rock. Although the red Staffordshire clay was ideally suited to the original purposes of the Potteries, as the wares grew more refined whiter clays were needed. There were ample supplies of these in Devon and Cornwall, and it was the need for a swifter and steady transport system both to bring in clay and to take out finished pots that led Josiah Wedgwood, with the help of James Brindley and the Duke of Bridgwater, to institute the Trent and Mersey canal to link the Potteries directly with the docks at Liverpool. No further proof of the astute business brain of the first Josiah is needed beyond the fact that he ensured the building of his great new pottery, to be called Etruria, on the very bank of the canal.

Once in the area, the fate of the clay became considerably diversified depending upon its destiny. It might need weathering, for instance; it would almost certainly require additives of some kind, perhaps calcined flint or other clays rich in minerals such as iron or felspar, or even the ground bones of cattle if the end product was to be bone china. It was not long before specialisation came to the region in the shape of millers who undertook to provide these additives ready for use, thus saving each individual potter the expense of setting up his own production. Once the clay and all its partners were safely inside the walls of a potbank (a group of buildings which included all the necessary processing facilities for the production of finished wares) the real game began.

The literal prime mover in the potbank was from the early nineteenth century a steam -engine sited in its own pit and connected by means of shafts, push-rods, gears and cogs to parts of the works often some distance away. The motive power was transmitted through all this mechanism and at the end of its journey was harnessed to turn wheels, move milling devices or stir vats in various buildings within the site. The engineman was thus himself an important cog in the machinery.

But the entire manufacturing process was governed by King Clay. From his body was made the substance of each pot and all else was merely cosmetic, depending on the variety of process chosen. Pots might still, as two centuries before, be thrown on the wheel by craftsmen using the skills of their many-times-great grandfathers; they might be shaped or hollowed by ingenious tools operating on lumps or "bats" of clay revolving rapidly on a wheel; they might even be turned like wood or metal on a lathe; or a newer process, that of casting, might be employed. Because of its readier adaptation to increased production speed, casting came into universal use. By producing a number of moulds from a master, the moulds themselves being made of a porous plaster material and having therefore a limited life, several dozen jugs or vases could be produced at the same time by simply pouring into each mould clay held in thick suspension in water and known as 'slip'. The absorbent drawing action of the plaster took in the water, pulling the clay particles in to itself to form a coating of clay on the interior of the mould. When the remaining liquid was poured off and the mould itself taken apart, there emerged the shape of the particular piece required, in a still soft but firm clay. When dried to what was known as a "leather-hard" state, the shape could be treated as though it had in fact been thrown from solid clay, have handles or other embellishments attached to it, be smoothed, fired and decorated.

Thus, of a pottery making domestic hollow-ware the slip-house was an important part in which there was a constant hum and clank of machinery and the interminable slop and slurp of solid clay, with its attendant additives, being mixed and cajoled into liquid form. The huge vats in which this transformation took place were in perpetual motion during working hours and often out of them, too. Other clay preparations intended for use in solid-state processes suffered compression in large accordion-like pleats which squeezed out all the liquid, but for the slip liquidity was its important property. From the slip-vats the mixture was generally conducted by pipe to places convenient for the filling of smaller vessels in use for pouring direct into the moulds. Simple, you might say, and you would be right; but there is nothing so clever as simplicity.

In the 1930s, in a potbank of medium size with three bottle-ovens around its yard, there worked a man called Ted Borrowcleave. His allotted and vital task was to oversee the operation of the slip-house, and this for fifteen years he had done with care and dedication. He was valued by his employers for his efficiency and application rather than for his brains, and he justified this confidence without the slightest hint of original thought. His thoughts were confined to the few non-working and non-sleeping hours which each day of his life magnanimously allowed him. These thoughts took in a certain amount of football, for he supported the local team which had worked its way up to participation in the national game at a national level.
They took in also a deep wound to which his innermost being had been subjected when the young lady on whom he had set his heart had walked off calmly with one of his boyhood friends. Ted paused not to consider the young lady's right to her own opinions and preferences, or the relative merits as a husband of himself and his rival. He nursed in his still-open wound a deep hatred of the other man, Frank Eversleigh. Even at school, though the two had been mates, Ted had been consistently eclipsed by Frank. When Ted played for the second team at football, Frank was promoted to the first. Let Ted gain high marks in an examination and Frank would promptly notch up a higher score. Even now, though Ted was in charge of the sliphouse, Frank was a senior foreman over the entire moulding and throwing department. Above all, Frank was married to Ted's girl.

On a Friday evening at the start of Potters' Holidays - the Wakes Week of the Potteries - most of the works staff had left rejoicing for their short stay in Rhyl or Llandudno or Beaumaris. Gradually the remaining men disappeared until only Ted and Frank were left, checking their respective departments to ensure that no vestige of a possibility of a problem remained to fester during the forthcoming closure. The engine fires had been drawn, the machinery was still, and in the sliphouse the vats contained only a milky fluid which would prevent the hardening of residual clay on their broad flanks. Ted was not going away - not because he was unable to afford to do so, but because he had not the heart to go alone among so many couples and families hell-bent on total enjoyment at any cost.

It was then that Frank committed two grave errors, one of which alone might have been expected to bring down retribution upon his head. It was bad enough that he had mentioned, with a definite hint of malice, how much he and Mary were going to enjoy their holiday. But to compound this with a veiled criticism of Ted's handling of the sliphouse was too much. Leaning over the side of one of the massive vats, Frank had reached down a hand and felt the liquid, and sniffed audibly in a tone of disapproval. Ted's hatred of this man welled up within his soul and exploded through his entire nervous system. With no real thought at all in his brain, his body leapt across to the vat, and smote the offending interloper on the back of the shoulders, toppling him head-first into the diluted slip. As Frank struggled, Ted's body reached out and held the focus of its hatred under the surface until the frantic thrashing ceased. Only then did Ted's brain start to work again.

He was not sorry for what he had done, except in that it would upset Mary, and he realised that he would be damned for ever in her eyes, never mind those of the law, if the scene which had just flashed by in his sliphouse became public knowledge. He pulled the body from the vat and laid it on the floor, which he still had to clean. With a hosepipe he washed away most of the traces of slip from face and clothes, and sat down to consider the situation. He felt little remorse - rather a curious sensation of achievement. He found, too that he could now think of Mary as an unfortunate episode from the past instead of a constant source of pain in the future.

After five minutes, Ted got up and went across to the crate-maker's shop, returning with a ball of twine. Looping this under the dead man's armpits, he lifted the body onto a clay-barrow and trundled it down to the edge of the canal which ran at the foot of the yard. Next door to the pot-bank was the wharf of a canal carrying company, and several of its towed barges, or "butties" were moored, encroaching in part onto the yard-edge itself. He carefully slid the body into the murky water of the canal, retaining the other end of the twine and, walking along the barges pulling the dead man after him, came to the opposite end of the wharf, where there was access onto a bridge over the canal.

The towpath in both directions was deserted. Even the usual anglers had departed to try their luck in the alien environment of the Irish Sea. Crossing the

bridge, Ted guided the body to the opposite bank, towed it some yards further away from the potbank, removed the twine completely and allowed the corpse to sink into the four feet or so depth of black muddy liquid .
From around a bend in the canal several hundred yards away came the sound of revelry. Ted knew that the canalside pub there would hold its customers until closing time, when they would come out in a noisy crowd and stagger along the towpath towards their waiting families. It was far from unknown for one or more men to fall into the canal and have to be hauled out by their jeering mates. A loner falling in, and no help within call, could easily lead to a tragedy.

Ted returned to the yard by the same route which he taken with the body. He washed the barrow and put it in its usual place. The twine he stuffed in his pocket to be burnt later. He finished cleaning the sliphouse floor, removed all traces of the struggle from the side of the vat and took final stock of the situation. He could think of nothing which might connect the body to a quarrel within the potbank, though he did accept the risk of enquiries being made as to Frank's movements after leaving work. He made the assumption that because no-one had seen Frank fall into the canal, people would think that he had not in fact been in a pub but may have stumbled accidently when sober but perhaps tired. He clocked himself out, waited for twenty minutes or so and then did the same for Frank.

The holiday week went by. Mary had raised the alarm when Frank had not returned home by late evening. The police went round to Ted's lodgings and established that he had left the works before Frank, a story which was corroborated by the clock cards. Enquiries from the local pubs revealed that Frank had not been seen in any of them. He must, therefore, have gone missing on his way home or possibly on his way to get a drink. His distraught wife, who did not yet know that she was a widow, did not set off for the coast on the following morning. Her mind was in a whirl. Had Frank left her for another woman? Had he had an accident? Or had he been taken ill suddenly? The police had no reason to drag the canal, and in fact never even considered the possibility. It was not until a passing barge brought the body to the surface that the mystery of the disappearance was solved, at least in part. The site at which the body had been discovered seemed to indicate that Frank had in fact been on his way to the towpath pub, as this was not on his normal route home.

The sad ripples of a tragedy appearing suddenly like a stone thrown into a pond spread remorselessly outwards from the desperate grief of the widow, through close family and friends to the outer limits of acquaintances, the local newspaper and ghoulish bystanders. Ted expressed formal sympathy to Mary and offered any help which she thought he might be able to give.

At the beginning of the following week, the potbank was back in full operation and a collection had been taken up for Frank's widow. It raised an amount roughly commensurate with his position in the potbank and the detestation with which the majority of his staff had come to regard his rather lordly approach and attitude to those whom he considered his inferiors.

Meanwhile, the normal police processes had been followed. The pathologist who carried out the post-mortem had confessed himself puzzled by the traces of clay which he had found in the lungs of the deceased. He mentioned this to the inspector in charge of the (at this point) ordinary investigation. "I conna say et maining out", said the inspector, but nonethless took the matter up with his superintendent, who in turn spoke to the fledgling forensic laboratory which had recently been set up to serve the area. It was arranged that a sample of the clay from the lungs should be analysed and an attempt made to establish just why it was there in the first place and whence it had come. The Inspector had many relatives who worked in potbanks. They told him that every pottery tended to have its own secret recipe for some of its clay mixtures, so he checked with the laboratory whether, if he obtained a few samples, they could analyse and match them. The answer being in the affirmative, the Inspector selected a dozen or so local potbanks and visited each of them with a request for a small amount of their clay. He received various ribald or derogatory answers, but after explaining a dozen times the reason for his request returned in triumph with his harvest of clay, solid or liquid and each item labelled with the name of its source.

Ted Borrowcleave, outwardly calm, supplied a sample from his sliphouse. Inwardly his whole body and mind were in a state of unimaginable turmoil. The unthinkable had happened. He had a great respect for the near-superhuman powers of the chemist and had no doubt that his sin would find him out. That evening his mind went into recession. Alone in the sliphouse he fashioned a noose out of his leather belt and his red-striped braces, climbed on a chair and flung the improvised rope over a beam, placed it round his neck and kicked the chair away. He left no note. Next morning his body was found, swaying slightly in the movement of air from the newly-opened door, and with the trousers around the ankles. One of his colleagues, a man with a vicious and macabre sense of humour, muttered to his mate :- " Power owd Ted. Haze oweeze bane a beltun breeces mon."

The police force found it difficult to cope with this second mystery and never thought to connect it with the first. It was assumed that perhaps Mary had spurned Ted's offer of help, or that he had forgotten to post a winning football coupon. In due course the report came back from the laboratory "Regret cannot help," it said. "Can find no significant difference between any of the samples, including that taken from the body." Within a few months the football season had started, Wedgwoods had been obliged to lay off a handful of staff, and war clouds were gathering over Europe. The twin mysteries were no longer news and only Mary remembered her husband and spared a kind thought for Ted Borrowcleave - successful murderer and sliphouse suicide.

CREDIT WHERE CREDIT'S DUE

Norman and Gerald had been friends since their days together in junior school. They had gone on to the same secondary school, left at the same time, and applied together for their first job. Both had been taken on as salesmen by a national firm in a sideshoot of the advertising business. As they very quickly learned, there were salesmen and salesmen, and the job they had undertaken was about on a par with trying to sell refrigeration equipment to eskimos. Advertising space was , and probably always will be, one of the most difficult things to purvey, mainly because on first sight it appeared to offer no concrete asset in exchange for hard-earned cash. And space in a local directory was even harder to get rid of. For a start, provincial businessmen usually thought that they were sufficiently advertised by their membership of the Chamber of Trade or the Rotary Club, and the majority of them had little faith in bold print within a vast tome of competing businesses.

It was well known in the trade that there were two ways of maintaining or possibly increasing the area figures achieved for the previous publication. One was the honest way - a painstaking coverage of each possible prospect, calling on every single address in every single street, and hoping for the law of averages to operate in your favour. The second was to employ the 'speciality salesman' technique, which essentially consisted of pestering the life out of a few prospective customers until they either threw you out or gave you a bit of business in desperation. It has to be said that the second method was not conducive to accuracy in the forthcoming edition of the directory, as many run-of-the-mill entries were not checked at all.

Gerald and Norman had consciences and used the first technique, for which they were rewarded, under the law of averages, by a string of increased area figures and the odd complimentary (though unaccompanied by monetary appreciation) letter from their sales manager. The pair stuck this life for several cities and towns before there dawned on them the appropriateness of an old saying - " there must be easier ways of earning a living." They discussed the situation one evening in a pub in Leeds. "The problem is", argued Gerald," that we aren't really trained for anything in particular." "And we don't have an ounce of technical knowledge or suchlike," added Norman; "So what do we have, or what do we know?" They pondered in silence. "We do know a bit about the directory advertising business", said Gerald; " have you noticed how often you find someone who seems interested in a bit of bold type and then backs off when you ask for the cash?" Very true," agreed Norman, "but how does that do us any good?" Gerald suddenly became animated - a relatively rare occurrence for him. "Supposing we offer these blokes credit terms?" "And how the hell do we do that", sneered Norman," I certainly can't see our masters in London printing stuff on tick and having to set up a load of extra accounts to keep track of what's owing." "Of course they won't, idiot", answered Gerald," but we could." Norman carefully took his pint away from his waiting lips and set it down gently on the table. "You mean,- put up the money, keep the records and take all the risks?" he asked. "Speculate to accumulate, Norm", came the answer. " Here's a plan, off the top of my head. Mr.X is interested in bold type worth ten quid but doesn't want to stump up the cash. So we offer him a small display for twenty and credit terms to pay it off. To quite a few people that will be irresistible. And how do we do it? To start with we'll need enough capital to cover a carefully computed amount of business over the first couple of months. Then we'll need a simple but foolproof accounting system. But most important will be the mechanism for collecting the debts. As far as the rest goes, the only difference is that we shall have to finance the credit part of turnover, but remember we get our commission share back the following month. At the same time we add on a bit for administration costs or interest, or things like that. Once the idea's been going for a few months it should be more or less self-financing".

Norman began to show a bit of enthusiasm. "You might have got something there, " he admitted. "What about collection of the debts, though. We can't ask for post-dated cheques - I think that's illegal- and we'll be off to another town before the loan is paid off, so we can't collect personally." I'd thought of that," Gerald went on. " Provided we have an agreement which also counts as an IOU, we can ask for payments (say six maximum) into our bank account and give out bank credit slips with everything pre-printed. Mind you, we might need to find out whether or not we need a money-lender's licence. And we would probably be advised to form a sort of club, perhaps with a token membership fee and certainly with an official-looking membership card."

At this point, the reader should remember that the time when all this was taking place was neither BC nor AD but BCC - Before Credit Cards - though, as it turned out, not long before. Savings clubs and Christmas clubs there were, and organisations sometimes rather shady which would lend you more than you had actually saved up.

Over the next few weeks, the plan was refined and improved until both of its sponsors were satisfied that there appeared to be no loopholes. "Our firm shouldn't object", said Norman "we aren't doing anything in their name - it's our money and our risk, and what goes on between us and our credit customers is our business. Besides, think how much more business they'll stand to get! But I don't think we'll tell them just yet!" So, in due course a new company was set up under the name:- Acrucana, Ltd., which stood for "Advertising credit you can afford".

"You know what", said Gerald one day, " I've been reading 'The Card' again. What about getting a patron." " 'The Card'?", queried Norman. "Certainly", came the reply. "Don't you remember the Alec Guinness film we saw a couple of months ago? That was taken from an Arnold Bennett novel, and I often re-read those. Denry Machin got the Countess of Chell to be patron for his Five Towns Universal Thrift Club". " Don't see the connection", grumbled Norman. "Ours certainly is no thrift club and we sure as hell don't know any countesses." "Negative! Negative,"scolded Gerald. "I was thinking we might get Fred Marples to become Chairman. A great ex-England footballer's name always looks good on a letter-head." " I suppose so, if he'll do it", conceded Norman.

And so it was done, and Acrucana prospered - rather to Norman's surprise. The money rolled in smoothly, with only an occasional bad debt. The business figures on every area undertaken by Norman and Gerald rocketed, until after a couple of years it was impossible to conceal their scheme any longer from their boss. The great man was surprisingly affable in an interview whose contemplation gave the two entrepreneurs sleepless nights. "Good stuff," he told them; "highly enterprising, well thought out and executed, and all done without in any way upsetting our business. It has done us good, in fact. I wish I'd thought of it myself, but I don't suppose you'll be wanting to sell out yet. I have absolutely no objection to your carrying on under those conditions. In fact, let me give you a tip. I understand that you've both recently got married. No doubt the thought of a few more nights at home will appeal to you. So you have my permission to recruit some of your colleagues to work for you, which should free you to concentrate on improving the administration side of your little set-up - which, as you'll probably agree, is still a bit Heath Robinsonish." The pair left the Presence almost walking on air.

Within a couple of months, they were both spending more time at home than away on the road and four eager youngsters were supplementing their standard income by carrying a different standard - that of Acrucana - with them on their many business calls.

"This deserves a party you know", said Norman one day. Both now had nice houses, adjoining, with good gardens and an interconnecting gate. Norman had married Ann, a small and extremely pretty brunette, while Gerald had committed matrimony in the company of Jilly, Ann's friend and as different as chalk to cheese; Jilly was a tall, beautiful, blonde. The four had met on several occasions at local jazz-clubs, before coalescing into an official and later permanent foursome. The party was cosy, business talk was barred, the food at one of the better restaurants in the neighbourhood was imaginative and the wine carefully selected by Gerald, who had taken the trouble (once he could afford it) to learn a bit about such things.
After the meal there was no argument about going on to a local jazz club, dancing the rest of the evening away and returning home arm-in-arm in a state (to put it politely) of heightened awareness and a mellowness which rapidly matured into excitement. The lights in the master bedroom of each house were not long going out, but that did not signify that the occupants were asleep..

A couple of months or so after the party the four were sitting over coffee in Norman's garden on a sunny Sunday morning, discussing progress and possible future plans. Ann seized on a slight lull in the conversation. "Speaking as directors of the company - junior maybe - " she said, "It may interest you to know that Jilly and I have been giving a good deal of thought to an entirely new credit concept. " Four male ears wagged visibly. "The floor is yours", answered Gerald, half-mockingly. "It's like this", continued Ann. "What would you say to a scheme which involved a relatively small cash outlay on deferred assets, double security, a repayment holiday for, say, six months, and a high rate of interest." "Sounds too good to be true", interjected Norman. "I fail to see how any scheme can possibly incorporate all those advantages. What about ownership of the assets, for instance, and what form would they take?" "You should have thought about that before you agreed to invest in it", put in Jilly. "Do what?!?", gasped both husbands. "We've signed nothing".
"Oh yes you have", chorused the girls; " and we can produce tests to prove it was your signature. You've already made the investment, both of you!" Jilly murmured to Ann - " it struck me as being more of a divestment, but never mind." "Let's see the proof, then " almost shouted Gerald. The girls stood up and together wriggled their still shapely torsos, rather like a pair of belly-dancers. "What's that supposed to mean?" complained Norman; Are you saying that we are part owners of some sort of shady dance-club?" "MEN!!!!" said the wives, in

derisive unison; "Thick as two short planks." "On second thoughts, perhaps not all that short", giggled Ann. She popped into the kitchen and produced from the cupboard a packet of disposable nappies. "Here's your first interest payment," she said.

Gerald and Norman sank stunned into their chairs. Had their knees not been in the way, their jaws would have shattered on the marble tiles of the patio. "Both of you?" groaned Norman, incredulously. "You'd better believe it," said his wife, throwing herself into his lap and her arms round his neck. "How about a bit of lap-dancing while there's still time?" Gerald turned to Jilly. "Do you take these new credit cards?, " he asked. "No dear," she replied; "Strictly cash. But the credit's all yours!"

THE LAST WORD

As soon as his feet touched ground outside the prison wall, Bill Bates knew that his luck was in and that his mates had done a good job. Crouching in the bare glimmer of light from the moon he ran silently for half a mile until he came to a ditch below a long thorn hedge. Pacing off thirty yards from a gate he descended into the ditch and uncovered the bicycle which had been carefully concealed under leaves and other vegetation. First emptying the saddlebag, he changed into the old clothes which he found in it, hid his prison garb under the leaves, pocketed a handful of notes and coin, mounted the bike and rode steadily down the lane towards the main road.

With an appearance supporting his inevitable sobriquet, "Bill" was largely forgotten and Bates answered generally to the name "Basher". This mirrored also the strong tendency to violence which had landed him in several prisons after robberies in which he had not been over-particular about the health of his victims. On this occasion he had sneered at the judge who sentenced him - "I'll have the last word, you prick". It was his intention now to leave the country and try his luck elsewhere.

The road to which he soon came was the northernmost of the main east-west Pennine crossings, and he planned to travel west, turn south on the M6 and make for Liverpool docks. A mile or so along the road he came to an all-night transport cafe, where he hid the bike behind some derelict huts and sauntered into the full, delicious smell of bacon whose traces had already reminded him that he was hungry. He ordered a large fried meal and went to a table at which a lorry-driver was just starting on his food. It was not too difficult to strike up a conversation, introduce the fact that he was anxious to get a lift towards the west of Scotland, and cement a deal by offering to pay for the driver's supper. The two men left together, and in the darkness beside the lorry Bates tapped the driver none too gently on the head and dragged the body behind bushes at the edge of the parking lot, where he rifled pockets to find keys, driving licence and other personal papers, which he transferred to his own jacket. Within five minutes he was on his way west behind the wheel of a large box-van whose scarcely-decipherable number plates read "STA967B". "My own initial. he thought. "Must be a good sign."

At exactly that moment, not far from Glasgow, a large car containing four tired young men was making its way steadily south. The car had started from the far north-west coast of Scotland, where a once-lonely and lovely sea loch was now an ugly industrial site as a vast construction of steel and concrete was rising higher and higher into the sky, threatening soon to overawe the purple mountains sheltering the village on the opposite side of the loch. This was the seventies, and the race for North Sea oil was under way. The despoiling of natural beauty was a small price to pay for the anticipated commercial benefits which could accrue to Scotland and to the nation as a whole. The car belonged to Peter, and he was driving. His friend Charlie occupied the front passenger seat and two other workmates were asleep in the back. Behind them was a long, roomy boot filled to overflowing with their gear. All four were returning to London for their regular week's break - on the rig they worked four on and one off.

Peter and Charlie had been living away from home for several months. On an impulse they decided that, before looking for a career, they would spend some time going round the country and getting to know more about their native land, its people and its heritage. They had pitched their small tent in friends' back gardens, in forest clearings, on remote hillsides and beside streams in torrential rain in Welsh valleys. Eventually, out of money, they had come to the loch where the oil-platform was just beginning to take shape and had applied for work. Having been told that they would have to wait for a month or so, they had survived on fish caught in the loch and on an occasional handout from the tough construction workers, who took both a liking to and pity on them. When the promised job materialised they had gratefully accepted the long hours and the rough conditions and had been taken on as assistants in the canteen where, at least foodwise, they lived like kings. They had made this journey a dozen or so times and always regarded Glasgow as a sort of watershed from which it was nearly all downhill along the motorways to London. They continued southwards through Ayrshire, eager to reach the northern end of the M6.

Seventy miles to the south a police Landrover was cruising up and down a long stretch of the motorway, pausing occasionally for a tea-break or to detour slightly onto a different road. Weather conditions were not good. There was more than a hint of fog in places and the temperature in October was already low enough for the droplets of moisture to freeze in the air and on the ground. The radio in the patrol-car burst intermittently into life, usually with some personal comment or simply to maintain contact. Until, suddenly, a note of urgency broke the tedium of the night-shift. The absence of Basher Bates had been discovered and a full gaol-break alert was broadcast. On a southbound leg of their interminable shuttle movement, while parked temporarily in a police lay-by, the two constables in the police-car were passed by a large car, not exceeding the speed limit but not exactly hanging about. Peter was an excellent driver but it was his car and he had no intention of either wrecking it or falling foul of the law just for the hell of it.

The Landrover pulled out, soon overtook the other vehicle and flagged it down onto the hard shoulder, parking in front of it. Any suspicion which the policemen may have harboured was not allayed by finding four young men in the early hours of the morning on this lonely stretch of road. Driver first, the lads were interrogated one by one. Their stories matched, their documents seemed in order, but the constables were not satisfied. Telling Peter to return to his vehicle they began to check out his story. Peter walked back, took his place again in the driving seat. The engine was running for warmth inside the car and occasionally a cigarette would be lit. The sidelights were on, but the fog was beginning to thicken a little. After about a quarter-of-an-hour, one of the back seat passengers suggested that Peter should make a run for it. "No way", replied Peter; "That's probably exactly what they're waiting for. They must be bored stupid on a night like this."

Nonetheless, he got out and walked to the patrol-car. "How long?", he asked . "You'll just have to wait", was the reply, and the other policeman added "Look out for the heavies." By now lorries in ones, twos, or groups were beginning to thunder past in the direction of Manchester, Liverpool and Birmingham.

Returning to his seat, Peter fiddled with the radio in a half-hearted attempt to hasten the all-clear. A couple of minutes later there was a huge bang, and the car was lifted simultaneously forwards, sideways and upwards with a groaning and shrieking of tortured metal and forced hard into the Landrover. Both vehicles teetered over the lip of the tarmac and dropped a couple of feet into the field below. The boot of the car had burst open and covered the carriageway with the pitiful debris of the lads' gear, forming small heaps smothered in diesel fuel. By merciful good fortune, neither vehicle caught fire, but Peter was trapped by one foot in the driving seat, Charlie was thrown clear on the other side,. one of the back-seat passengers passed out momentarily before staggering out, bleeding from a nasty cut on his forehead and the other lay unmoving, pinioned between front and rear seats.

The two policemen, basically uninjured, crawled back up up the bank to find that a lorry had come hurtling down the hard shoulder and ploughed into the back of the car, slamming it in its turn against the rear of the Landrover. There was no doubt that both vehicles would never travel again on their own wheels. In their haste to get out, the constables had missed an urgent "all-cars" call reporting a possible connection between the gaol-break and the theft of a lorry.

They were, however, able to summon help immediately. They next checked quickly on the lorry-driver, who was dazed and suffering from a crack on the head. The score was thus:- relatively unhurt -3; wounded -3; seriously injured -1. It was obvious what had taken place. The lorry-driver had fallen asleep for a split second and lost control of the vehicle. He had recovered quickly enough to avoid doing anything stupid like running off, and a quick check of his documents satisfied the constables for the time being. The group waited for help to arrive. The front of the lorry was seriously crumpled, but the legend on the number plate at the rear could be discerned through the thick mud and dust with which it was be-spattered. It was STA967B.

Half-an-hour later, all four of the young men had been taken off to hospital, with the prospect of a grilling by the police after treatment. It was already nearly morning on a day on which anxious parents, shaken by the non-arrival of their sons and later devastated by telephone calls bringing news of the disaster, would race up the motorway to collect three of the injured and what remained of their belongings. The fourth had survived, but would be in hospital for a long while and would probably never work again. The ambulances gone and the carriageway cleared sufficiently to allow traffic to move normally again, the various rescue and other police vehicles dispersed.

Meanwhile the driver of the lorry had been taken by the original officers back to a local police station. There he was now inwardly congratulating himself on coming successfully through the ordeal of a somewhat perfunctory questioning and examination of documents, which were superficially in order to the casual eye. The station sergeant, with instinctive misgiving, gave him permission to leave, on the basis that he would certainly be required for further questioning in a few hours time. He was sober, and many other drivers before him had fallen asleep at the wheel. But there would be at least a query about excessive driving hours to investigate. Meanwhile he was free to go, on leaving an accommodation address. This was conveniently supplied by the name of a pub visible through the window of the police station.

Bates walked towards the door exulting quietly to himself. Transport was temporarily a problem, but there was more than one way of killing a cat. The sergeant's eye fell suddenly on two reports laid out side by side on his desk, and that eye, sharpened by years of police experience, by an instinct for things which did not feel quite right, and by the bristling of hairs on the back of his neck in the presence of villains, registered a fact which took yet a few seconds to be transmitted to his brain. On each report was a vehicle registration number, and the two numbers were the same. The sergeant was used to acting on instinct and to the rapid addition of the the lowest even number to itself. "Hey, Basher!" he called out. Bates paused and turned his head. "What?", he answered. He had, after all, had the last word.

WITCH

The world, from the beginning, has been in broad terms classified, dissected, explained and formalised into the four constituent elements - Air, Water, Earth and Fire. Around these four has grown up through several millennia a mythology which has varied from global personification into four master-gods to the invention of large hierarchies of minor deities serving each all-pervading idea. It is the latter system which has provided posterity with a rich folklore in which each deity has as many names as there have been cultures and often a considerable variation in capabilities and attributes, into the bargain. For Air - Hathor, Dyaus, Shu, Juno, Uranus; for Water - Poseidon, Neptune, Sarasvati; for Earth - Tiamat, Geb, Privithi, Demeter, Ceres; and for Fire - Hephaestus, Loki, Vesta; and that is to name but a few.

To exist, a hierarchy must of course have lower ranks, and thus the mythology expanded to embrace many minions for each master. Among these, imams and priests, lamas and rabbis, gurus, witchdoctors and vestal virgins evolved to personify at the lowest level the divine authority of each of the prime elementals. Not the least among the ranks above these acolytes in the Western world were the witches. Much has been written about the mixture of awe and abhorrence in which the human witches of the middle ages were held, but this tale is concerned more with their superiors, who were a great deal closer to the masters and served them directly without regular human contact, though it was their custom to assume, both for convenience and for effect, shapes which men had come to associate with the concept of magical power.

The main executive servants of Air were the Wind-Witches, one for each quarter of the compass - North (the leader), East, South and West. It was their custom to meet at a central point to receive instructions directly from their master, to bring him information gathered in their travels and to discuss with him any action suggested by recent human events. For the remit of the Elementals was not only the care of the physical world, but also the guardianship of the essences of humanity among its vast and widespread population. Many an apparent accident of nature occurred to protect a single human being whose destiny was important, or to direct the progress of events which, turning the wrong way, might change the course of broadly-ordained history.

At a certain date towards the end of the sixteenth Christian century, the witches received an urgent summons to a meeting in equatorial Africa. Their progress,

as usual was rapid and cautious, so as not to alarm the denizens of the countries over which they passed.
The Witch of the North travelled swiftly southwards.

> On her broomstick rocking, high on the crest of the wind the Wind-Witch
> came, riding the deserted streets of the sky.
> Black her tall, needle-point hat and the tattered wisps of her cloak,
> but blacker the brilliant sheen of her black witch's cat.
> Far southward she fled, fast borne on the cold north air,
> and the bare tops of the tall trees leapt in the gale as she passed.
> To the shore of the ocean wide of dark wind-cloud she came,
> and fields and naked woods slept as the fierce wind died.
> The ragged clouds drifted, heavy with snow, and lighly, unhurried
> as the faded trees in autumn, let fall their crystal leaves on the brown
> world below. The night stole by, while myriad flakes eddied down
> over the slumbering village,
> and the silent stone church watched, saintly beneath a soft, bright crown.

Far to the south a grave company listened to the breathy words of Air. "Ladies", he said, " a certain danger threatens the small island over which you, North, must have flown on your way here. In some three-hundred-and-fifty world-years from now, that island will be required to stand alone against a shadow of evil which will seek to destroy this rather pleasant globe. I cannot take risks with its continued existence at this point in time. Let me explain, briefly, the situation, which is due to one of these many petty squabbles which we have consistently observed amongst men - usually to do either with some sort of territorial ambition or dispute, or else with the ridiculous rivalries between adherents of different sectarian divisions of those who seek to align themselves with us. As you know, these people consider us (quite correctly) to be of divine power and majesty, and they believe that, properly petitioned and propitiated , we shall advance their cause regardless of merit. Broadly, and to an extent, that approach can work, but any such considerations must be subordinated to our need to follow the dictates of destiny, which after all we have ourselves taken the trouble to create."
"In a few months, when the spring season is well established, a vast fleet of their frail wooden constructions will embark on the intervening sea, carrying a huge army of warriors whose task it will be, once safely delivered, to subdue the island nation. Personally, I don't think they can do it, but I am not here to take chances. So, I am trusting you to make sure that this fleet does not reach its

destination. Use what means you like, within reason of course, and you can count on the active help and support of the servants of my elemental siblings. You have my full permission to consult and plan with them as you think necessary. But you had better not fail or there will be a few unexplained accidents occurring to broomsticks in transit. Best of luck, and keep me posted of developments at all times." Air faded gently into non-presence.

"Right", said North. "How are we going to do this?" "Easy", replied West. "We just blow their ridiculous bits of wood until they either sink or break on the rocks at the edge of Ocean." "Don't be daft", chipped in South, "whatever we do has to look like an accident. I suggest that we liaise with the sand-spirits of Earth and the wave-wraiths of Water. Together we can surely come up with something convincing." "Count me in on that,", said East, " and it might be worth while bringing in the flame-fairies of Fire as well; you never know when they might come in useful." "Agreed", ruled North. "A type of combined operation. Sounds good to me".   The meeting ended with a resolution to meet again, on site this time, a month later.

Morning arose in a light of silvery grey. Snow, and the stillness unbroken hovered, motionless, dazzling white. And out of the South, as the new day was born, flew a dark figure - the Wind-Witch northward returning under the gates of the dawn. Her moon-shadow flitted past tower and parapet, and the red roofs of the houses and the grey stones of the street thrilled under their glistening coverlet.
Near, and nearer she sped, a weird, lonely figure with only her cat to keep her company, and the tall hat on her head.
The chimney pots, roused as she deftly unfurled the blazing banner of dawn, knew not she had talked with her three sisters at the ends of the world. Along the first sunbeam swiftly she flew beyond their circle of sight, and the dull clouds in the morning sky parted, revealing a mantle of misty blue.

On May 29th, the great Spanish Armada set sail from Lisbon, one hundred and thirty-six ships carrying nearly twenty-two thousand soldiers. Each fighting-ship carried stone cannon-balls and wildfire as an opportunist weapon. As the fleet rounded Cape Finisterre and came towards the waters of Biscay, the wind-witches marshalled the forces of air and sky and called down a great storm, which quickly chased the hapless mariners back to land, where they sheltered for a month to repair damage and recover their nerve. A small Island fleet sailed with the intention of giving battle, but decided that discretion was the better part of valour and wisely returned to port to await the enemy's next move. In fact, the delay caused by this apparently premature action on North's part served to disrupt the too-rigid plans of the invaders, and several of the ancillary armies which were to support the landings were thrown into a certain amount of confusion.

The Island fleet was more numerous than that of the Spaniards, but very much smaller in average unit size. West, with her experience of sunnier climates, said that it looked to her as if the conflict would be reminiscent of gnats attacking bumble-bees. Events were to prove her right, and she executed a little plan of her own by providing favourable winds which drove the Armada into a great patch of fog in the northern part of Biscay, where she promptly stopped blowing altogether and the resultant calm caused much of the fleet to lose station and disperse. By the time they had reformed they were at the entrance to the Channel, where their presence was immediately reported to the Island commander. Then and afterwards, the Island propaganda machine worked overtime to such good effect that the bringing of the first news of the Armada's presence in Island waters has found its way ineradicably into historical legend.

Just as West had predicted, when battle was joined the Islanders buzzed around the unwieldy and crowded vessels of the invader like gnats. Their greater speed and manoeuverability enabled them to dart in and out amongst the larger ships, delivering stinging blows without harm to themselves. Meanwhile, a quiet word to the flame-fairies had set them to destabilising the wildfire so that it would burst into flame at the slightest provocation. And still the West wind blew, until suddenly another calm fell on the two fleets as they were within sight of the great white rocks at the western tip of a satellite island off the coast. At these rocks were gathered some of the forces of Earth, watching the progress of the battle with a view to setting their strategy for a future phase of the operation. Meanwhile, on land, the decision to mobilise the defending army was taken. Over the length and breadth of the island there appeared, one after the other, a great series of beacon-fires designed to spread the news of imminent danger. Come wind or rain, the fires proclaimed their message, protected by the small attentions of another contingent of flame-fairies.

Nearly three hundred years later, the Island poet Macaulay immortalised this operation in stirring if somewhat blatant verse:-

> For swift to east and swift to west the warning radiance spread -
> High on St Michael's Mount it shone - it shone on Beachy Head.
> Far o'er the deep the Spaniard saw, along each southern shire,
> Cape beyond cape, in endless range, those twinkling points of fire.

While the battle-fleets lay thus becalmed, dramatic events were taking place some miles to the east, where another great host of ships lay in Calais harbour waiting to transport across the narrow straits yet another army. This too, however, was in some disarray due to the delays already suffered and the consequent interference with original plans. These plans were destined to receive another, much more disastrous setback.

Eight small boats could be seen, approaching from the west the great harbour crammed with vessels of all descriptions. West the wind-witch was blowing them gently along on a calm sea. At a given signal the crews of these boats set fire to the large piles of combustible and explosive materials which had been gathered on decks and in holds. They then jumped for their lives as the fires took hold, fanned by the slight wind and tended by another group of flame-fairies. Inexorably the small flotilla, impelled by the gentle breath of the West wind, bore down upon the immobilised fleet, pinioned down like sacrificial lambs. A fire-ship struck, and then another, and soon more. As the anchored vessels caught fire and their cables burned, they in their turn joined the stately choreography of death as it claimed new partners at every figure of the dance.

Still the wind blew, increasing in strength, and the becalmed ships of the great armada began to move again, ever to eastward away from their homeland. Goaded by the stings of their small, agile opponents, these vessels found themselves drifting into shallow waters, where these were not expected. Could it be, perhaps, that sand-spirits had deviously played fast and loose with the bed of the sea and thus caused ships to run aground? In despair, the stricken fleet turned northwards with the wind which now veered slightly to blow from the south.

They ran soon before an increasing gale along the eastern coast of the island which their leaders had vowed to conquer, round its northernmost tip and into an area of an untold number of small islets, large rocks and treacherous seas. At every mile along the way vessels vanished beneath the waters which were heaped upon them by attendant wave-wraiths. Others found in the midst of apparently clear sounds sudden upthrusts of jagged rock which pierced hulls and shattered skulls until no trace remained of ship or crew. Closer to land, the cliffs put out in gestures of dersion tongues of granite whose tips fastened on to struggling ships and drew them, chameleon-like, back to the waiting rocks of the shore. Ships and crews gave themselves up to terror and despair.

Turning south by now, the remnants of the armada, completely scattered, fled homewards still pursued by the vengeance of the elements. A few lucky souls managed to reach the shore alive, but not all these escaped the wrath of the inhabitants. Weeks later, singly or in small demoralised groups the armada came home, unrecognisable as the proud fleet which had set sail four months previously.

The Island breathed deeply and offered thanks for its deliverance. To its brave sailors thanks were indeed due, but other recipients of this gratitude accepted it under false pretences. This did not matter to the Elementals. Their wind-witches, wave-wraiths, sand-spirits and flame-fairies in one gigantic combined operation had successfully obeyed instructions and ensured that at least for the next four hundred or so years destiny would run true and the world would survive according to plan. North thanked the leaders of the other parties and prepared to return home. "Well done, girls, " she said to East, South and West. " We showed 'em!"

She turned to mount her broomstick. Something seemed to be missing. "Where's that cat ? " she enquired, looking round. "Blow me if she hasn't sneaked off somewhere" The other three let loose a huge gust of laughter. "Whoooooosh", they shouted together and tumbled North off her broom into a clump of bushes, from which erupted a yowling and howling as of several thousand devils. Out from the vegetation stalked two large cats - North's and West's. Behind them, tails up and paws moving with almost military precision, came two jet-black kittens with brilliant emerald eyes.

"You dirty slut!" said North, as the kittens sprang to her shoulders and their parents appeared to be arranging some future rendezvous. "Aren't they just adorable", gasped East and South, who had no cats. North's cat fixed her mistress with a scornful stare. Saucily she grinned and silkily she spoke. " So nobody else is allowed to engage in combined operations, then? Jealousy will get you nowhere! Besides, we were only doing your sisters a favour". She waved her paw at the kittens, who leapt from North's shoulder to the respective broomsticks of East and South. " Behave yourselves", growled their parent. "Yes, mother," replied the kittens, purring;" we'll take good care not to do anything you wouldn't do!"

Four broomsticks, each carrying a satisfied cat, took simultaneously to the air and flew off in different directions. "Wait till I get you home", said North to her familiar. "Keep your hair on", came the throaty reply; "it's not exactly a catastrophe, you know."